Watching the Wind Blow

Sara Alexi is the author of the Greek Village Collection.
She divides her time between England and a small village in Greece.

http://facebook.com/authorsaraalexi

Sara Alexi

WATCHING THE WIND BLOW

oneiro

Published by Oneiro Press 2014

ISBN-13: 978-1505314496

ISBN-10: 1505314496

This story is based on real events experienced by a member of my family in the year 2000. Names and dates and characters have been changed, but the basis of the events described is true. I would like to thank them for their openness in telling me this tale.

Many thanks to Alex, Lori, Susan and Tony for their invaluable help in proofreading this book.

Chapter 1

There is a delicious cool bite to the air this early in the morning. Pink tinges in the sky promise the dawn but for now, the enclosed stone-flagged courtyard is in shadow, the wisteria gently hissing as the morning breeze scrapes it against the whitewashed wall.

Inside the stone house, where yesterday's heat lingers on, everyone is sleeping. Even Angelos, his tiny mouth hanging open, twitching into smiles as he sleeps, clutching 'Bun-bun'.

Within seconds, the pink hues of the sky pale overhead, giving way to the most delicate of blues, and there is just enough light for the urns, cascading with geraniums, to cast their shadows against the courtyard walls. The smell of jasmine drifts with the breeze.

Irini, in the courtyard, stretches, her yawn becomes a gentle growl, and her eyes shut with the intake of breath. Through the open window upstairs, a snort is followed by a creak of springs. Petta sleeps on. A heavy sigh lets Irini know, before the snoring begins, that without her curled up next to him and

3

nudging him, he has turned on his back. A twisted smile softens her face as his sonata begins and, refreshed by the fresh air on her skin, she goes back into the kitchen to make coffee.

The brown walls of the kitchen do little to reflect light. The cream door of the fridge and the white marble top of the old table glow in the gloom. A gecko clicks to its mate in the roof beams. Switching on a lamp set in the wall spreads an orange glow over the immediate surroundings. The table top, and, to the lamp's left, crude wall shelves, the front edges of which drip with cobwebs of lace, all fall into high relief. By comparison, the rest of the room has grown darker, introducing hidden corners; doorways into darkness. Below the bottom shelf, casting shadowy fingers, hang bundles of rosemary and oregano that have been drying out through the summer for winter use, their aroma leaking into the room as the air is stirred.

One of the doors from the kitchen opens to a corridor that leads to the front door, which is usually left open. The door halfway along to the right is that of the *kalo kathistiko*, a formal sitting room that has the comfort dusted and polished out of it. The other door from the kitchen leads to the room that Marina insisted she take as her bedroom when Petta and Irini moved in, giving over the two upstairs bedrooms to them and the then-unborn Angelos.

'No steps. Better for my knees,' Marina insisted, bending to lift a sack of rice to be weighed into smaller bags for the shop.

4

Lighting the single-burner camping gas stove that sits in a well-stained area of the marble table top, Irini waits for the water to heat in the little copper *briki*, then adds the sugar and stirs to help it dissolve. A basket beneath this table holds a stack of unpaid bills, and is at the point of overflowing. Waiting for the liquid to become clear, Irini uses the time to put back in one or two red-topped letters that have floated out onto the smooth-painted concrete floor. The paint is wearing off in the most well-trodden areas, but really, the whole room needs a fresh coat of paint. It's not going to happen soon. It will have to wait until the bills are paid first.

Irini reflects, and not for the first time, on the irony of the family's financial situation. Marina has money, and quite a lot of it. Most of it is tied up in an investment which seemed like a good idea at the time. Since the crisis though she is standing in line with a lot of others trying to get back what she can from the beleaguered investment company.

'You will get the money back, don't worry,' Babis the lawyer assured her, although the furrows on his brow suggested otherwise. 'But this is Greece,' he mused, 'and legal processes take time. We will have to wait for the court process to conclude.'

Some of the money is in the bank, a not inconsiderable sum. 'You will not touch one drachma of that!' declared Marina, 'It is Angelos' inheritance.'

'Euros, Mama, not drachmas.' Petta, unconcerned by their plight, seemed to find the situation infuriatingly funny.

'Euros, whatever. That money is for Angelos to go to university, and you will not spend any of it.' And she clattered off to the sink, banging the pots.

Irini suspects that the real reason Marina does not want to use any of the money, which was given to her, and not earned, is not so simple.

Marina built up the business that now struggles to sustain the family from nothing, after her husband died.

'I have never been rich,' she will declare, 'but I have always been happy. Well, nearly always... There are many rich people who are not happy.'

Marina's life, her identity, and her position in the community are based around the corner shop. If she admits to herself that she is wealthy, that she does not really need to work for a living, that would change her standing with the people she has known all her life. Presumably that is too great a sacrifice, a leap too far into the unknown. Meanwhile, the bills demand to be paid.

The gas hisses in the silence; Petta must have turned back onto his side. Once the liquid is clear, she adds two heaped teaspoons of grounds from a foil pack. The powder sits on top, slowly absorbing the water, until, with a plop, the remains of the coffee mound disappear beneath the surface.

The foil pouch is replaced on the shelf.

Irini takes down a postcard propped on the shelf next to the coffee and reads it through again, for perhaps the hundredth time, and shivers slightly. Today! After how long? She cannot even remember how many years; it will be wonderful to see Stathoula, no matter how briefly. There's no avoiding work this morning, but she has cleared the rest of this day of the usual mundane chores that eat up her time. Even Marina, who always seems to need a lift somewhere - this last week visiting her neighbour who is in hospital for a hip replacement - does not need to go anywhere, and Angelos has no play dates or parties to go to. She is free. Today is for Stathoula. Stathoula and her.

If anything extra comes up at work today, she will be firm with the old captain and will not stay longer than her appointed hours. It is not as if he even pays her for the extra work she does, sneaky old man that he is. Irini sighs. At least she does have work. That's something to be grateful for, with things as they are and so many unemployed.

Compared to the norm, today will seem leisurely. An unexpected chuckle escapes her.

The snoring upstairs begins again. The rafters, thick beams of wood overlaid with bamboo and then floorboards on top, seem to shake.

Thoughts of Petta have such power that her chest feels tight and her stomach twists. It is a different feeling than she has towards Angelos. What she feels for Angelos makes her catch her breath. She never dreamed of such a luxury as the love she has for him. He is an indescribable part of her that fills her with unashamed pride. Even at this young age, she knows her time of being the centre of his world is brief and, before she has caught back her breath, he will be spreading his wings and creating a family of his own and, no matter how strong her love is, she will let go, not because she wants to, but because it is what he will need. But Petta, he is her rock, immovable. From him, she is inseparable.

A gentler snoring comes from behind the door off the kitchen. How lucky is she to get on with Marina as well? She is pretty sensitive for a *Pethera*, and God knows she has heard some terrible stories about her friends' mothers-in-law. But their history is short. Even her history with Petta, rich as it is, only spans a few years, and there are some things which she has left unsaid, bits of her history that have remained unspoken. When they first met, sometimes it felt as if Petta did not want to know everything about her and sometimes, she has not wanted to dirty their relationship with the things she has seen, emotions she has felt. Maybe a part of her did not believe that he would understand, not having lived the life she has.

That time seemed to pass so quickly; the beginning of their relationship when they shared their histories and got to know each other seemed to speed by and still, certain things were left unshared. Perhaps she worried too much that she would damage the image of herself that Petta seemed to have in his mind. In the end, rather than bring up details of her past again, it became easier just to let things slide. Besides, there just never seemed to be the right moment...

Now, just going about their day-to-day lives, these unsaid things become even more difficult to say. Now they weigh her down, a gulf Petta doesn't even know exists. A chasm which separates her from not just him but everyone else in the world.

If she reaches out to Petta, maybe the gap could be closed. But what if their fingertips could not touch? What if she is unreachable? There's the fear.

Whereas Stathoula and her sister Glykeria knew her when her parents were still alive, knew Yiayia before and after that day that changed her. They were at her yiayia's funeral together and they were just as dry-eyed as she was. They all knew, knew what Yiayia became, understood who she was before. Yes, maybe she could talk over all that again, maybe even open up about a little more about being left on her own and all that happened. They had wanted to know back then, when they took her in, but Stathoula was also sensitive and she did not ask questions; instead, she just let Irini take her time. And Irini had wanted to look forward, not back, and so has never really spoken about how things were for her. Besides, her throat had tightened every time she tried to speak out. But now the time seems right, and it would feel so good to have someone listen who can really understand. Maybe Stathoula would be as keen to hear now? That would be good. More than good! So much of what she keeps hidden is becoming increasingly heavy. It's time to exorcise that piece of her life. Stathoula will understand.

The bubbles in the *briki* break away from the edges, the foam gathering to form a reef in the middle. As the aerated coffee begins to rise to the top, Irini lifts it gently from the heat and pours the contents into her waiting cup. Some spills onto the ageing marble-topped table and she mops it up with a cloth from the sink. She throws the cloth back and almost misses. It hangs from the edge.

She listens for the sound of anyone stirring. Is that a faint murmur from Angelos? With the luxury of time in hand, she leaves her coffee to settle and creeps up the stairs and into the first room on the left to stroke Angelos' hair, his dark curls raven on the pillow. His whimpering subsides in a gentle rhythmic breathing at the feel of her touch. Irini kisses him lightly but lingeringly on the forehead, and it is only with effort that she can break this contact, tearing herself away from his smell, his warmth. To compensate for her absence, she pulls the light blanket around his shoulders, tucking him in, and closes the crack in the curtain to keep out the morning light, allowing him to sleep for longer. Blowing him another kiss, she returns downstairs. Petta is still snoring.

Outside, the sun has lightened the whole sky. Although the orange globe is not yet visible in the courtyard, the west wall is topped with its yellow rays. Birds begin to cheep and chirrup in the trees throughout the village and the chill has gone from the air. The cicadas are warming up for their day-

10

long hoarse chorus, and their volume increases as the minutes pass and the day's heat takes hold.

The dividing line between day and night creeps down the wall towards the ground as the sun rises in the sky, lighting up both the flowers and weeds that grow out of the cracks between stones and crevices in the whitewash.

There is the slightest settling of dew on the table that stands in the courtyard beneath the lemon tree. Wooden legs scrape across the flagged floor as Irini pulls a chair out to sit. Not having to think about a million tedious jobs that keep the home going and the corner shop running for a day is a rare luxury. The coffee tastes good, its sweetness lifting her energy. The sun peeps over the east wall and filters through the lemon tree, mottling her t-shirt. Maybe she should be going? Would it be pushing it to take the time for a second cup? The sooner she starts, the sooner she will get back.

'Rini?' The grunt of a sound comes through the upstairs window.

If she had left earlier, she would have missed Petta's waking. Maybe if she is quiet, he will think she has gone.

'Rini?' The grunt becomes more formed. The sound of his voice is enough for her to yearn to run back upstairs and slide under the blankets to curl up in the safety of his embrace. But if she does that, the day will never begin and today of all days, she must set out and get home early. Irini finishes her coffee noiselessly and puts the cup down carefully on the saucer.

If she goes back through the house, he is bound to hear her and call again. He will want a coffee, then Marina will wake and she will want coffee. Their noise will wake Angelos and then there will be crying as Irini tries to leave, Yiayia Marina holding him back, tempting him to play with something. No, it is better if she goes through the other door, through the shop and from there into the street. Also, she can grab a pre-packaged chocolate croissant from the rack by the counter on her way through. Her stomach grumbles.

She steals across the courtyard and pushes open the back door to the shop and closes it carefully behind her. The front window and doorway to the emporium are so crammed with wares for sale and colourful promotional stickers that Marina loves to paste on every surface that little light gets into the shop, even at midday. Now in the half-light of dawn, the shop is dark. Clusters of candles hanging from the rafters click against her forehead. Stepping to one side to avoid them, her foot catches a bundle of shepherds' crooks that are stacked by the back door, and as she puts her hand out to steady them, she knocks what sounds like packets of mothballs off a hook in the wall and they land on the floor, crunching underfoot as she moves.

'*Re gamo…*' The expletive is on her lips but she stifles it before it is fully formed, freezing, listening to see if Petta heard. She waits. There is a

12

scuttling in the courtyard, a mouse or a lizard maybe, but from the house there is silence. She exhales.

If she stays to tidy up, the time will march on. She will also have to turn the light on, which would probably wake Petta. No, the best thing to do is to leave it. Marina will clear up the mess if Petta doesn't.

The shop door opens onto the village square. A cockerel crows, but the rest of the village is asleep. The kiosk in the centre of the square by the palm tree is still boarded up, as it is left every night. The chairs and tables from Theo's kafeneio are stacked and chained to the telegraph pole. Even the tiny sandwich shop that opens early to serve the children on their way to school and farmers on their way to their olive groves is dark. There is a dim glow from the bakery, but its doors are still firmly bolted.

A cat runs across the square, tail erect, ears forwards, and disappears into the shadows. The cockerel tries to rouse the village and a dog barks in irritated response, but nothing else stirs.

Searching her pockets, for a moment, Irini thinks she has forgotten her car keys. As her shoulders slump and she sighs a breath of defeat, she suddenly finds them and her energy is restored. The smell of fresh bread plays in the air. The baker and his wife, or more likely their son-in-law, will be the only people awake in the village at this time of day, preparing the staple for the trickle of customers that will filter through their shop from when they first open their doors until late morning when every last loaf has been sold. Irini's stomach grumbles again as she throws the croissant onto the passenger seat and climbs in herself.

The newsreader on the radio drones her monotone syllables. Something about the police being shamed, a prisoner escaping, and a suburb of Athens up in arms that their neighbourhood is not safe now with such a man on the loose. The police spokesman comes on, reassuring, insisting they will soon catch him again. The weather girl's voice almost sings in comparison, over-enthusiastic that the day will be hot again. Irini clicks it off, preferring the silence.

On leaving the village, she changes gear and speeds up. The mountains in the distance are still black against the sky, which is now quite light. The orange trees on either side of the road are still all green, the oranges not yet ripe enough to show colour. The September rains have already started with a brief storm, warm rain and thunder the day before yesterday, soaking the ground enough for the roots to suck up water to plump out the oranges. It should be a good season. Perhaps it will take some of the pressure off, let Petta get back to the oranges and olive groves and her back into the shop. She can stop this early morning job that takes her away from Angelos. Maybe if the season is really good, it will even bring the prices of the oranges up so they can pay off some of the loan Marina took out to rebuild the shop.

But for now, it is lucky that at least one of them has regular work paying a steady wage. Although, she reflects ruefully, she is still owed some of last week's money. With a sweep of her hand, she clears shop receipts, sweet papers, and a baby's comforter from in front of the fuel gauge. That would be all she needs, to run out of petrol, but the needle shows a quarter and she relaxes and sweeps the rubbish back in place. The road to Saros stretches before her.

The little stone houses dotted between the trees become more frequent as she approaches the outskirts of Saros town. These give way to two-storey houses and then three-storey apartment blocks as Irini drives into the centre. A right turn takes her down to the port, where she parks with a handful of other cars and jumps out.

The sea lays like silver oil in the harbour, still and thick. There are one or two pillows of fluffy clouds low on the far horizon but the day, even at this early hour, is already warm now, and within the hour, it will be hot and it will be airless and sweaty below deck.

Boats of all sizes and shapes line the harbour walls. Towels drying over their booms, forgotten bikinis hung next to fenders, wine glasses abandoned amongst a mess of ropes, and shoes in the cockpits. Irini walks along, looking into each of the bobbing white boats, and she wonders if the tourists within give any thought for who clears up after them.

Chapter 2

Captain Yorgos is awake and sitting on the deck of *Artemis*, a thirty-foot sailing yacht that has seen better days. He is smoking his first cigarette of the day and his face is still puffy with sleep. He rubs his hand over his thinned, almost bald crown. He needs a haircut. The few strands of hair remaining create a fluff over his dome that stand upright and begin to look comical if they get too long. He is wearing a pair of dirty, baggy jeans and his distended stomach hangs over, covering both belt and zip. He slaps a hand on this taut expanse when he spots a thin man with a flat wooden tray balanced on his head, walking along the quay.

'*Kalimera*, Toli. How are we today?' The captain's voice is loud and authoritative with a patronising edge.

'*Yeia sas,*' Toli greets the captain. As they are about the same age, there is no real reason for Toli to use this polite form instead of the more relaxed *Yeia sou*.

Yorgos listens to Toli describe his morning so far, one hand holding his tray steady and the other gesticulating and occasionally pulling down his white shirt that rides up under his raised arm. The captain waits for him to conclude before indicating he wants a *koulouri* from the tray.

The sight of the *koulouraki* seller reminds Irini that she has left her croissant in the car along with her phone and she stops abruptly, ready to retrace her steps. The sun is bouncing off the sea's surface, so bright she screws up her eyes.

'Ah there you are,' the captain shouts from the cockpit of his yacht. Even with half-closed eyes she knows he is addressing her. Reluctantly, she gives up the thought of her croissant for the moment but she will need her phone for when Stathoula calls later. She can go and get it as soon as the captain has left, as is his habit, for coffee in the square.

'*Koulouraki*?' the man asks her and, reaching over his head, retrieves a circle of crisply baked bread from his tray and hands it to her, pulling down his shirt once she has taken it from him. Irini's free hand goes to her pocket for money which she knows is not there; this will be her excuse to go back to the car now. There was some change in the ashtray. A seagull flies high overhead, briefly passing between her eyes and the sun.

'I'll just go back to my car and get...' she begins.

'Put it on my tab,' the captain says to the vendor. If she goes now, the boat might not be cleaned in time for his clients. Was it six today? All

17

Swiss. He makes a mental calculation. Six times the fee, it will be a good day. Addressing Irini, he adds, 'I owe you a little bit from last week, so that will make us more or less straight.'

'Well, I, er…' Irini stutters. Surely it was five euros from last week and the bread ring costs, what, about fifty cents?

Captain Yorgos stubs out his cigarette and lights another. Picking up his peaked captain's hat and slapping it onto his head, he begins to heave himself up from his seat. His legs seem to get worse every day. The doctor told him to walk more after they put the stent into his femoral artery, but what does the doctor know of the pain he feels? They know nothing of the hardships of living on a boat, up and down the steps from the saloon to the deck every few minutes. It's even worse in the winter, when the boat is on stilts in dry dock and he has to climb a ladder from the ground all the way up to his cabin home. Besides, if those doctors had done their job right, why does it still hurt?

'You still owe me,' Irini states, just loud enough for him to hear as she concentrates on her balance across his homemade gangplank. She always makes it look like the thing is unstable. Some of the top layer of plywood has broken off here and there, but that coat of white paint has covered well. Look at her, holding tight to the handrail even now, when the sea is flat calm.

He is particularly proud of his ingenuity with the handrail. When his income is so uncertain, it is best to be frugal. Finding those pieces of domestic copper piping just thrown away in a skip at the boatyard was a great piece of luck. Such a waste, people throwing things like that away. Anyway, it has done him some good, as it gave him the idea of mounting them vertically at intervals along the gangplank with bungs of hand-whittled wood in the top of each, with holes drilled through to thread the rope from one stanchion to the next. Look at her grabbing it. If she pulls too hard, one of the bungs may come out.

Toli turns to leave.

'Hang on. You going up to the square?' He addresses the bread seller, who grunts but for some reason does not look too happy. Never mind, he will cheer him up. 'Give me a minute and we will walk together.' Standing now, his belly feels taut and he wheezes. Everything is a struggle these days. Pulling on a faded shapeless t-shirt that advertises a brand of decking varnish completes his outfit.

Irini steps to one side of the helm to give him a clear pathway to the gangplank.

'New bed sheets for my cabin today and yesterday's clients cooked. Italians.' He emphasises their nationality as if it is an explanation. 'They wanted pasta, so they cooked. The galley's a mess, as we hit a bit of wind just before lunch. Oh, and can you stay on and clean all the glasses? Some of the ones I took out yesterday had fingerprints on them.' He looks about him for his lighter, which Irini spots first, standing upright in the centre of a coiled rope. 'The bareboat will be out today, so just a check over to make sure everything is still clean. Give the toilets a pump and put some bleach down them.'

'Did any other cabins get used on this boat yesterday?' Irini asks. She cleans the boat Captain Yorgos lives on every day, but as he only uses it for day trippers, the cabins seldom need attention unless someone feels seasick and needs to lie down. Captain Yorgos' other yacht, tied alongside, is hired out as a bareboat, and the holidaymakers captain it themselves. It can be gone for a couple of days or as long as two weeks. That vessel only needs cleaning occasionally but when it does, it takes hours and hours, from scrubbing the deck to cleaning out the bilges. Last time, it took all day. If Captain Yorgos would pay her a fair hourly rate, those days would make a good impact on the situation at home.

'A child lay in the front cabin for a short sleep, but I would not called that used.' He is looking around again – for his glasses, Irini presumes. She looks too and spots them for him, hooked in the neckline of his t-shirt.

'Ah, yes, right, now I am just popping out. Some business I need to attend to. Also, can you make a list of anything we need to buy? Window cleaner, cloths, that sort of thing. You may have to go shopping.' Irini opens her mouth to protest that this

20

is not part of the job she has agreed to do but before she can say anything, he is talking again.

'Right, let's go. We'll wander past the port police if that's alright by you?' He addresses Toli as he swings on a stay to go around the helm. Slipping his deck shoes on his bare feet, he rolls his way down the gangplank, which creaks its resistance.

He is getting too old to be doing this job, Irini reflects. If he was a younger man, all the half-finished jobs would be completed and he wouldn't spend so much time sitting in the square drinking coffee.

Going down below deck, she gags at the acrid smell of stale smoke. The galley is filled with pots that have not been washed, spaghetti dried onto surfaces, pans black with baked-on sauces. The ashtray on the chart table is full and this is the first job Irini decides to tackle, emptying it into a carrier bag she finds on the floor. The gentle rock of the boat feels familiar; she quite likes the movement but the stale air is more than she can bear. She opens the saloon hatch and then, grabbing the wind-scoop from the shelf above the chart table, she goes up on deck to tie this piece of curved material to the boom and the edges of the open hatch. What little wind there is now will be caught and blown below, refreshing the air in the cabin.

There are a few people about now. The cafés on the front are all opening. Their tall doors show off their high ceilings. Some are rich with ornate scrolled wood around chamfered, etched windows; others are chic and simple with chrome handles on tall frameless glass, doors that are invisible when closed. Clean-shaven men in tight shirts sashay between tables, putting out ashtrays and menus, assured of their days' pay and tips.

The sea has turned from silver to a transparent blue and over the side, she can see shoals of small fish darting into the shadows under the hull. On the sea bottom, the rocks are pocketed with dark sea urchins too deep to spike careless feet. A single, larger fish glides into the shadow of the boat, creating an explosion of little fish darting back into the sunlight. She must take Angelos on a boat trip. He would love to see the sea life.

Reluctant to return below until the air has cleared a little, Irini judges what there is to do on deck and, kneeling, she takes hold of a mass of rope and, lying the end on the deck, starts turning it with the flat of her hand on top. The rope coils around itself, lying close to the deck where no one will trip over it. It is satisfying work and she continues with all the ropes until the deck is bejewelled with flat rope spiral snakes. She won't swill out the cockpit until she has finished the other jobs, knowing her own footfall will create mucky marks as she brings rubbish and mop buckets and anything else that needs to go up or down the saloon steps and out to the bins on the quay side.

She opens a locker under the cockpit seat to see what a mess the life jackets and beach toys are in, and takes a few minutes to tidy them. She will not wash it out today. In fact, with the bareboat needing so little doing to it and relatively little to do here, this could be a really short day. If she can finish and leave before the captain comes back, that will also save some time. Closing the locker lid, she sits on the cockpit seat and looks out to sea.

Stathoula and Glykeria. In retrospect, it was obvious that they would be at Yiayia's funeral, but somehow it was a shock to see them there. She found herself unable to meet their stares. Her life had been so rough since her parents died that just the sight of her cousins brought a memory of softness, comfort that somehow made her feel so far away from them. The tears in her eyes were from the joy of seeing them, the tiredness from her way of life. But then, when you are fifteen, how else do you live if you have no home, when you have no one? Putting it that way, it's amazing she was at the funeral herself that day. How different her life might have been if she hadn't bumped into the stall holder.

The yacht rocks as a fishing boat putt-putts past. The mountains that enclose the bay have colour now, brown and greens fading to pale purples in the distance. Somewhere over those mountains, Stathoula will be driving from the airport on her way to see Glykeria and her new baby down in Kalamata, Irini's village almost exactly the halfway point. But just a lunchtime stop seems such a short time.

No doubt Stathoula will thrill over Angelos, but what will she make of Petta? If the wedding had not been such a spontaneous affair, she could have met him then. There is no concern, though. She is bound to like him; everyone does. But he is not exactly in the same league as Stathoula's husband, from what she has heard. A German, like her father. The days of hand-me-down clothes may be long gone, but their positions have not changed.

That was her chief memory of being with Stathoula and Glykeria when she was little. The girls turning up in a new car, Mama greeting Dierk, her brother-in-law, and his new Greek wife warmly, always a sad look on her face as she remembered her sister. Irini on strict instructions not to let slip that Glykeria's birth was the cause of her aunt's death. But Irini knew that they knew anyway, which made her wonder for whose benefit they were not allowed to talk about it. So the topic was avoided and they played in the field, Irini happy, Stathoula and Glykeria enjoying the freedom, getting dirty.

Those visits came with clothes that Stathoula and Glykeria had grown out of, and this was exciting when she was tiny. After plates of *briam* and glasses of homemade wine, Yiayia had helped her dress and undress, trying on the pretty things that were so unsuitable for playing in their field. But as the years passed, the clothes mostly served to highlight the widening discrepancies in their worlds. The visits slowly became less frequent, and each more pocked with repeated explanations to Yiayia about where her second daughter was. In her confusion, Yiayia began to accuse her son-in-law of terrible things, and the

24

visits stopped soon after that. That was around the time she started digging random holes in the field.

'*Mana mou*.' Irini's own mother addressed Yiayia. 'She died in childbirth. She was not even in Greece, let alone near here when it happened. Remember?'

Yiayia's starry eyes stabbed holes in her as she glanced about.

'*Mana mou*, come inside. I will tell you again. She married Dierk. You remember Dierk the German? They had Stathoula and then there was a problem when Glykeria was being born?'

Thunk. The *tsapa* dug deep into the soil and Yiayia used all her strength to lever open a hole. Thunk. The *tsapa* excavated deeper.

'*Mana mou*, come let us make some coffee,' Irini's Mama coaxed.

Yiayia never did quite seem to understand. Mama and Baba became worried about leaving her on her own when they went off to the markets and Irini to school. Irini would regularly return to find little excavations pocking the field, sometimes uprooting crops. Often, Irini would cover over the worst if she was back before Mama and Baba, just to try and relieve some of their worry.

Then the day came that Mama and Baba would never return and that soon after Yiayia began to wander off as if searching for them. Irini mostly caught her before she had gone too far, but some days, Yiayia could be very sneaky and Irini would find her streets away, completely lost.

The fishing boat leaves the bay and the rocking of the boat settles. If she is going to see Stathoula today, she'd better get on. She must put the pots that need washing to soak and pump the toilets to clear out the stale water and, while the bleach acts in them, she can nip back to the car for her phone.

And then one day, Yiayia was gone and could not be found. It wasn't long after that that the field and the house were repossessed by the landlord. That hollow sinking weight of being left with no one and nothing settled into the pit of her stomach, becoming a part of her. That feeling stayed until Stathoula took her in.

Below deck, the air has cleared a little. It is not so acrid. Above deck, it is hot now, but below is even hotter. She opens the door to the forward toilet. Water sloshes below the duck boards, and the soap suds from people taking showers make everything look grimy.

If ever there was a good day to be caught for stealing! That market stall holder had no idea of the favour he did her. The police were involved but it turned out to be good luck for her that day.

The sink, which has yellowed with age, is always impossible to make look clean, and someone has left a toilet roll out whilst using the cubical as a wet room and the soggy tissue has disintegrated on the side.

It turned out the stall holder had known her parents. But it was the policeman who linked her name with the old lady they had found. He told her about the funeral before releasing her with a reprimand but still with no place to go and no food to eat.

To a great extent, it was the memory of all the food at her parents' funeral that persuaded her to go to Yiayia's. It certainly hadn't occurred to her that her family had been traced and that she would see Stathoula and Glykeria.

On the shelf above the toilet and below the porthole is where the first aid box is kept. Really, it is a thick plastic sandwich box with the words '*Artemis - First Aid*' written in indelible felt pen. It has been opened and the contents are spread out on the shelf; there are tubes in the sink and sealed plasters on the floor. An empty shampoo bottle is in the tiny bin which hangs on the back of the cupboard door below the sink and this stops the door closing and the one into the room from opening fully. Irini is unable to get into the space and she fishes about until she retrieves the bottle. Once in the room, she opens the porthole to let out the smell and heat.

That was what had hit her first about Stathoula and Glykeria's house. The cleanliness. They led her first to a bathroom with a free-standing bath on legs with big industrial-looking taps.

That initial feeling of sinking beneath the warm water was such a luxury, she thought she might never climb out. Stathoula and Glykeria left her alone, and she marvelled at her luck. She did not want to soil their world with her own experiences. She wanted to embrace her new life and her cousins. Cast off the street. Forget the horrors she had seen. Lock it all away, pretend it had never happened.

It was a natural thing to do, even if not the best. If only she had found her tongue back then, talked to them, told them about the time between losing her parents and their Yiayia's funeral. Talked about it all when it was fresh rather than letting it settle, bury its way into her, become a part of her, stagnating.

Maybe talking today will help loosen some of the armour she has put up. Let people in a little closer?

But just a couple of hours at lunch is not even enough time to give all the thanks she needs to give Stathoula, let alone talk. Still, if she only stays for a couple of hours, an hour even, or just five minutes, enough time to see her face, feel her embrace, it will be a moment of completeness, an acceptance, an absolute joy.

Besides, now that she is settled, maybe they can find ways to see more of each other. Kalamata's not so far to see Glykeria. Even Germany these days is only a few hours on a plane. She could get a passport.

The toilet is flushed by using a hand pump, and Irini pumps vigorously, drawing sea water into the bowl and back out again into the sea. It gushes and rushes through unseen pipes. As she is pumping away, the first aid box shifts from its place on the shelf by her head and she struggles to push it back. The lid has come off and something inside jams it open. The water in the toilet gurgles and for a moment, Irini doesn't hear the new noise. But as she stops pumping, she can hear a definite throbbing and the duckboard beneath her feet seems to be juddering. It is as if someone has switched on the engine. Things from the first aid box rattle out and a tube bounces off the toilet seat and onto the floor. Maybe Captain Yorgos has forgotten she is on board. Could he be back already, with day trippers? It's a little early. If he casts off now, he may be reluctant to put her back ashore.

As she backs out of the toilet, the first aid box falls onto its side by the sink and she bangs her hip against the door handle. Wincing and bending with a hand covering the pain, she rushes to the steps that lead up to the deck.

'Captain Yorgos. Hey Yorgos, have you forgotten I am on board? Don't cast off.'

Chapter 3

With the light behind the figure streaming in from above deck, Irini has no idea who or what she is looking at. Initially she thinks it is Captain Yorgos, his arm outstretched, handing her something, and her hand twitches in response to accept the offered item. But there is something in the way the person moves and the steadiness of the hand that holds the object outstretched towards her that makes her hesitate and take a step back.

The figure fills the space at the top of the steps. Irini takes another step back as the glare lessens, and the figure descends one step. The object is still held out, the shape becoming real. The round black hole at the end of a shaft lined up with her forehead. His grip unswaying around the handle. His cheek level with its sights, suggesting images from films. Irini gasps, sweat breaking into beads on her forehead.

'Who are you?' the gruff voice asks in a clear English.

'*Kanenas*,' Irini's voice croaks in Greek, generating a flick of incomprehension on the man's face. She repeats herself in English 'No one, a cleaner.' She vaguely lifts the cloth in her hand as proof. The saloon blurs but she dare not move even to wipe her eyes. Coloured spots dart in her vision and she feels slightly sick.

He looks about himself, quickly, animal-like. In the aft of the boat are two cabins and a toilet, accessed by doors on either side of the steps that lead down from the cockpit. He pauses on the next step, reaches to open the door to the cabin on his left, releasing a stench of stale smoke and heat, male sweat and dirty clothes. A quick glance, his eyes only leaving her for a fraction of a second. Transferring his weapon, he opens the door to the other cabin. The bed lays smooth, made up with clean white sheets. Irini notices a corner that has not been tucked in, and at the same moment registers a fly that has landed on the frying pan soaking in the sink in her peripheral vision. Still on the stairs, he opens the door to the toilet next to the cabin and closes it again. Between these brief glances, his unblinking eyes stay fixed on her. The muscles in her legs seem to be weakening. Her mouth is dry. Her tongue has stuck to her palate.

Transferring his weapon back to the hand that it sits more comfortably in, he takes the final steps down and plants his feet firmly on the wooden floor. The saloon suddenly feels very small. Raising his free hand, he points with one finger. Irini's limbs respond of their own accord; a tremble runs through her. The finger is alongside the barrel, lined up with her head.

All his focus is on her. He is so still. He seems to neither breathe nor blink. His eyes are all black. Like a shark's.

'Open it.' He enunciates crisply. His finger still points. With sudden awareness, Irini realises he means the door behind her. She opens it, grasping at the handle twice in her haste. Another bed, freshly made up, ready for clients. Maybe with a wrinkle or two, perhaps where the child slept yesterday.

Angelos! If anything happens to her, what will become of Angelos? With this thought, her mouth creates too much saliva. She swallows once and then again. The cabin blurs all the more and this time, she cannot resist swiping a hand across her eyes, clearing her vision.

'Close it.' The voice is not unkind. Irini closes both the cabin door and her mouth. 'Both,' he adds. His finger now points to the door of the bathroom that she was about to clean before he appeared and the cabin opposite with twin bunks that is always open, used as it is as a general dumping place, and a store for bed linen, mop and bucket. She pushes every door shut.

The man seems to relax, inasmuch as he takes a breath and blinks. His eyes flick around the saloon, from the cleared table to the full sink, taking in the chart table where navigational charts are stored and the panel above that controls the lights, the VHF radio, and the other electronics on the boat.

'Stay below,' he says and then turns his back on her and skips up on deck. The engine's throbbing grows and Irini can feel the movement of the boat. The engine revs, causing her to grab the edge of the saloon table to keep her balance. There is no doubt that they are underway, but Irini cannot make sense of what is happening.

After what feels like forever hanging onto the saloon table, the revving is decreased and her legs can hold her no more. Is he alone? Are there others? Three rocking steps take her to the rear of the saloon. From here, looking up to the patch of light at the top, she can see him behind the wheel.

'I said stay below.' His words are shouted and she listens for the footfall of others overhead. Through the thin windows in the superstructure, she can see no feet. He is alone.

She will not do anything stupid. Images of Petta and Angelos bring her hand to her heart. If this man's intention is to shoot her, he would probably not do it below deck as a bullet through the hull would be a problem, wouldn't it? If she goes up on deck and he shoots her there, then he can throw her overboard and that's that. It is best to stay below deck.

The radio crackles - Captain Yorgos leaves it permanently on, mostly for company, she suspects. Right now, it is more than company: it could be her lifeline. It is only just audible over the throb of the engine, even where she is standing next to it. Irini's breath comes in short gasps. She glances nervously up at the hatch and her chest heaves. From where she is standing, all she can see is blue sky and the end of the boom swinging. She waits. Will he come down? The engine has found a steady rhythm, the boat rocks this way and that, never the same twice. Another glance through the hatch. He is standing and holding onto the helm, eyes far out to sea. She walks backwards to the radio and cautiously surveys the switches and knobs, one eye on the hatch. She turns the one marked volume way down low and then takes her time to think.

Captain Yorgos will sometimes run the engine to recharge the batteries and even when he has shouted to her down below, she has heard nothing. Likewise, she has shouted up to him on deck and he has not been able to hear her, and that was with the engine just idling.

She turns the volume up click by click till she can hear some crackling.

Irini's chest heaves like it will explode, but the hatch remains a square of blue. Lifting the microphone slyly to her mouth, she presses the button to talk.

'Port police, port police, this is *Artemis*. Come in please?'

Even though the man will not be able to hear, she dare not raise her voice above a whisper. She releases the button and waits. Silence.

'Port police, port police, this is *Artemis*. Are you there?' Releasing the button, she wills a voice out of the speakers.

'*Artemis*, is that you, Yorgo?'

'Er no,' Irini begins and then remembers she has not pressed the 'speak' button. 'No, this is Rini, I clean the boat for him.' The quiver in her voice must tell them everything.

'What can I do for you, Rini? Need some more bleach? Where's the captain?' There is a general chortle of voices over the airwaves.

'There is a man on board with a gun. Over.' She doesn't breathe, her heart stops beating. She tries not to blink. The situation becomes real in the telling.

'*Artemis*, did I hear you right? A man with a gun?'

'Yes.' Irini keeps looking at the speaker. 'He has taken the boat by force.'

She waits. The fly eats yesterday's bolognese sauce from the edge of the frying pan.

'*Artemis*, this is the port police. Over.'

It sounds so loud. She hastens to turn it down.

'Yes hello,' she whispers hoarsely.

'Rini is that you? Over.'

'Yes.'

'Have you seen his hands? Over?'

'I haven't noticed his hands. What about his hands? Wait.' She puts the microphone on the chart table and moves toward the hatch, staying out of the line of sight. At the steps, she ducks down and then raises her head in stages to see over the top. He's looking behind, back to Saros, his hands on the helm.

Smothering a gasp, she ducks down and creeps back to the radio.

'The end of his little finger is missing, ragged skin.'

There is silence. The wait seems to be forever. Raising the microphone to her mouth, she is about to press the button to talk when she hears,

'*Artemis*, he is a known mercenary. He is wanted for travelling with illegal documents. Dangerous. We will come. Try and keep in contact but do nothing to upset him. Do you hear? No heroics.'

The saloon is swimming. Irini wipes across her eyes with the back of her forearm.

'Leave the radio on. We will come.' The radio crackles and goes quiet. Irini slowly hangs up the microphone.

'Come up where I can see you.' He shouts the command from the top of the hatch. Did he see her, did he hear her? Will he just shoot her when she goes on deck?

Chapter 4

The steps up to the deck have rounded handrails made of teak. The treads are of thick plywood, the ends of which have been steamed to curl up at an angle. Irini has wiped over the non-slip rubber treads on their tops many times but, staring at them now, she realises why they are shaped so. If the boat heels over in the waves, in either direction, the sections at the end would be horizontal enough for someone to mount them easily. She notes the detail of the design as she puts her foot on the bottom step.

She has not wiped them over today. The day she had planned will not be and her bottom lip quivers. Petta will be awake and clearing up the mess she made in the shop by now. She wishes she had taken the time to make him coffee, tell him that she loves him, and cleared the mess herself. If she had, it would be Captain Yorgos at sea with this … this … this pirate! A little whimper escapes her.

The sun seems blindingly bright after being below for so long.

The pirate is standing, legs wide at the helm, a small Karrimor rucksack on the floor beside him, eyes focused on the horizon. Both his hands are on the wheel; the skin hanging where his little finger should be is even more gruesome close up. There is no sign of his weapon, and this gives her some relief.

As she stands on deck, Irini quickly checks the land on either side and realises they have made little progress. They are heading out to sea but only now are they passing the village on the coastline. Angelos will be sitting on Marina's knee in the courtyard, being fed his breakfast by now. The sun is overhead, everything dappled in the shade of the lemon tree, his little chortles pushing half-chewed food down his chin between mouthfuls. The cats will be rubbing around Marina's ankles, anticipating spillage. Looking back, she can still see Saros port, but there is no sign of the port police.

The man shows no interest in her. Her breathing becomes more steady. She is not going to die, at least not right now.

Hopefully this man, this pirate, just wants to go down the coast a little. If not, where is he heading? In time, they will come to the end of the deeply inset bay and the land will fall away on either side. If they turn left, they will go to Orino Island or past it to the Cyclades, Turkey, Israel? If they continue on their course, they will head for Crete or beyond to Libya; turn right and they will eventually hit Sicily or bypass it and head out into the Mediterranean, toward the straits of Gibraltar and through to the Atlantic. All these places are ridiculous distances. How far are they going? How long does he plan to be at sea?

Her stomach turns and a slight reflux burns acid in her throat. She must stay calm. She moves slowly and quietly to avoid his attention and sits on one of the cockpit seats. With her head down, she picks at a black mark on her jeans. It is probably oil. If she can pretend to be casual and friendly, maybe he will relax with her. There's oil on her hands, too. It will be from the engine, which nestles under a cover behind the steps to the saloon. Captain Yorgos is always tinkering with it, leaving oil stains all over the boat for her to mop up.

Try to be friendly, that is the best idea, calm and casual.

'Where are we going?' It seems harmless enough to ask, and just asking the question makes her feel like she is doing something. Sitting passively is not her nature.

He does not answer immediately, but frowns slightly as if deciding whether to reply. The question has obviously unsettled him and he shifts his weight from one leg to the other. Irini wonders if she should have not said anything, forced herself to be silent.

When she and Petta moved in with Marina, Petta took over tending the olive groves and fruit trees. When Angelos was born, Marina spent more time in the house and less in the shop, to take care of the cooking and looking after Angelos. Because of her youthful energy, Marina said, Irini would be better than her at running the shop. So Irini sat, day after day, serving the odd customer, with little to do, certainly during the afternoon's *mesimeri*, when most people were asleep, and so she began to keep accounts. It didn't take long to work out that what was brought in by the shop, and what little was earned by the orchards with the price of oranges so low, was not enough to keep a whole family going. It wasn't that the shop was doing badly - it was ticking over well and would have provided for Marina and would even have slowly paid off the loan she took out to rebuild it after the storm.

But on being reunited with Petta, Marina's heart had been, perhaps, more generous than her circumstances allowed, which Irini could understand now she had a son of her own. However, with more mouths to feed and Angelos growing out of his clothes every month, there was just not enough coming in.

Accounts were not something Petta would have ever thought of doing. The chances are that none of them would have noticed the shortfall until it was too late. But Irini had learnt the hard way to survive and trusted herself and only herself, so even when she found out about the shortfall, she did not tell Petta or Marina immediately but instead considered the problem for some time.

'Marina?' Irini had slipped out of the shop, through the courtyard, and into the house. Marina was in the kitchen making bread with Angelos. He was standing on a chair and had an apron on that hung all the way to the floor. Marina stood behind him, guiding his hands in the dough.

'Hi Irini,' Marina grinned, the skin around her eyes creasing into a thousand soft wrinkles. 'Angelos is a master baker today.'

Irini leaned over and kissed one of his floury cheeks. His eyes were shining with the fun he was having.

'Clever boy,' Irini addressed him, and his floury hands left the dough and came up around her neck for a hug. 'You'll put flour all over me!' She feigned horror, which made him laugh and wiggle his fingers at her.

'Well, it needs to be left to rise now so it's time to wash our hands, Angelos,' Marina encouraged. Washing hands proved to be an equal adventure, and bubbles took over from the flour, the flagstone floor slippery with flour and water. Irini briefly popped back to the shop when she heard the doorbell jangle and, after selling a packet of cigarettes, she asked Marina to take over for an hour. Angelos knew the shop as the source of sweeties and he was running across the courtyard before his hands had been dried, and before Marina had a chance to reply.

'Just an errand I have to run,' Irini explained.

Finding a job in Saros was not the easiest task. The cafés and tavernas needed no one, and nor did any of the tourist shops. Wandering the streets, the sun was relentless and despite the relative lack of greenery, the cicadas were noisy. Every request for work that was met with a rejection pushed at her patience, but most irritatingly of all, the tourists in front of her all walked very slowly. She was almost at snapping point when she stopped at the kiosk on the front to buy a bottle of water.

'Hot again,' the woman serving said, looking up at the cloudless blue sky as if this were unusual for Greece in September. They do say that after August it's winter, *apo Augousto xeimonas*, but the rain in September is always warm and this year, the summer seemed to be continuing forever.

'Yes,' Irini agreed, unscrewing the top of the cold bottle and wiping her forehead with the back of her hand. 'I don't suppose you know of any jobs going, do you?'

'Funny you should say that. Captain Yorgos,' she pointed across to a rather grubby-looking yacht moored by the harbour wall with a sign on a pole saying *Come Sailing, Day Trips*, 'was looking for someone for regular work, but only part-time, I think. But watch him, as he will try anything to keep his money in his pocket.'

At dinner that evening, Petta came in and kissed her on the cheek and sat next to his son and gave him a green orange no bigger than his thumbnail to roll around the tray of his high seat.

'Petta, how much time do you really need in the orchards?' Irini opened.

'Not much, really. I am still learning, but they grow themselves.' He chuckled at his joke and leaned over to pick up the tiny fruit Angelos had thrown on the floor.

'So if you had to do a few hours in the shop, that would be alright?'

'Yes of course. Why? Is it too much?' Suddenly he was alert, protective.

'I just thought a little change might suit us all. You could take over the shop in the morning, which would give me time to do the little job I have got myself in Saros.'

Marina's silence was audible. She came from a generation of women who did not talk back to their husbands nor do anything without their permission. Certainly she would never have gone out and got a job without her husband's consent when he was alive.

'You got a job?' Petta asked. 'Why?' and so she told them, presenting both the problem and then the solution. The money she would earn would slowly pay off the loan, leaving the income from the shop and the orchard for food and clothes. They would be fine now. Petta listened intently, with a slight frown, but then he looked at her with loving eyes and told Marina what a marvel he had married.

A seagull calls high overhead.

Irini rubs her hands together to try to get rid of the oil.

'Casablanca.' The pirate finally answers her question in a monotone voice.

Irini thinks he is joking and smiles to prove she is friendly, to collude with him.

'Why are you laughing?' His knuckles holding the wheel go white, all except his little finger, where the skins flops loosely as the wheel moves with the waves.

'Oh no, sorry. I didn't realise you were serious.' She scans his face, reading for signs of how much she has offended him. He has a generous mouth with curved creases in the corners. Lines from grimacing? Or maybe, at some time, he has smiled a lot.

'Why would I not be serious?' There is no smile there now.

'Well yachts are slow and Casablanca is on the coast of Morocco, right?'

'How long will it take?' He is very serious but perhaps he is offering her a chance to show she can be useful to him. It would give her some value in his eyes, which can only be a good thing.

'Here to Orino Island, which is the first island we will pass, will take eight hours just with the motor.' She looks him over as he concentrates on the sea, which is flat calm this early in the morning, with no wind for sailing. His jeans have seen better days but his dark grey t-shirt is new. Printed on it in black is a jumble of English words. She can make out a capital letter S and the acronym a.m. over which a pattern has been stitched in red cotton. It tells her nothing about him, but the colour choice seems to endorse his aggressive stance. His boots look like army boots, and they are scuffed and unpolished.

'When they bring the new boats from France, it takes about a week. But Morocco is further, so two weeks maybe?' she offers, recalling Yorgos telling stories of his younger days when he would deliver yachts to far-flung destinations.

'Two weeks!' He looks left and right at the land and then back to the way they are going.

It never occurred to Irini as she sat learning English at school all those years ago, or more recently improving it by watching American films on television, that she would need her second language for this. There is irony in there somewhere but she cannot put her finger on it. She shakes herself out of the safety of her musing. Right now, she must think, be even more alert than the pirate is, use this English to keep herself safe.

'Well, with good wind, maybe less. Although…' She is not sure whether to say any more. She wants to stay helpful, useful, but not negative.

'What? Say it.' Presumably realising that standing stiff-legged at the helm is not necessary, he sits, one hand still on the wheel and his back still straight. He has wide shoulders, narrow hips. The physique of someone who has done a lot of swimming, perhaps. A gull flies above them, its feathers ruffling gently. It is a young gull whose chest is still mottled. The boat moves off course slightly and the gull is silhouetted black against the sun.

'Well, I don't suppose we have any water in the tank.' Irini watches his face to see his reaction. 'Captain Yorgos usually rings the water man on a

Tuesday and he comes about the time I am finishing to fill up, and I doubt there will be any bottled water.'

'What day is it?' he asks. Her eyebrows raise. Is this a joke or is he serious?

'Tuesday.' She is about to add that the fuel man does not come until she is halfway through her cleaning each day either but decides that he does not need to know this. Maybe running out of fuel and the port police catching them up would be the best outcome. 'Also, there will be no food, as Captain Yorgos buys it every day depending on how many clients he has.'

The colour changes in his cheeks and the muscle there twitches. His eyes are green.

'But we can stop at Orino Island and stock up.' She tries to sound cheerful. Orino Island is where Petta was born and where they lived together for a year before they moved in with Marina. Orino Island, so safe and close. She grabs at her heart through her t-shirt, as she mouths the word *Petta* to herself. Tears prick her eyes and her hand slides from her chest to twist the ring on her finger. She catches the pirate watching her.

'Are you married?' she blurts out, almost accusingly. Hasn't she read somewhere that it is best to become a real person to your captors? Read where? In a magazine in their corner shop? She would give anything to be back there right now.

'I do not want to tell you.' Cold, emotionless.

'Oh.' She hadn't expected that and could never imagine saying something so blunt to anyone.

Her sights rest on one of the ropes she coiled earlier and the realisation comes that she will not be there to see Stathoula today. She cannot stop her bottom lip quivering; her vision blurs. In fact, with this man wielding a weapon, she might not be seeing anyone else on any other day, either.

The thought that she may never see loved ones again sucks her dry. Her head drops and her arms become limp and for a minute, she is boneless and motionless. The sun continues to shine and her body responds. The sweat drips from her forehead, making dark circles on her jeans which dry as quickly as they are formed. Something twists in her chest, and for a panicked moment, she wonders if she is having a heart attack, but then her fists clench, her mouth sets hard, and one side of her upper lip curls and twitches. The rawness of her emotion frightens her. The shadow of life before Stathoula and after her parents died passes over her. A memory igniting long-buried responses. She survived that; she will survive this.

She sighs a long out breath and her stomach settles and her fists unclench. The layers in between that time and this fall away. Her life with Petta, although the most important thing that has ever happened to her, recedes. Angelos, and the love she never believed she would feel, is neatly packed away, a velvet curtain drawn over him. Stathoula's successful attempt to build up her trust and belief in the world evaporates, and her eyes widen with the ease at which it all drops away and she is emotionally transported back in time. Nothing she has learnt since seems useful here, today.

She is the child again, the person she was from fifteen to eighteen – blasé but with adrenaline coursing, living by stealing, one eye always open, sleeping in hallways. Fighting with police and other street children. Avoiding Omonia Square where Indians and Pakistanis squatted in misery to sell mechanical toy rabbits with red glaring eyes. Whoever was forcing them to do their bidding was the enemy, to be watched for. There too were the Eastern-block men, quick to pull displaced people into their windscreen washing 'services' that were inflicted on drivers at red lights, a rap on the window and a hand out for spare change. But Omonia also felt like the centre for all homeless people and she found herself drawn to it again and again in search of company, to stop being lonely. A sharp eye and quick feet kept her safe from the pimps, the drug addicts and the police.

She can almost feel the stiffness of the grime returning to her hair, which she has never allowed to grow long since. Easily remembered are the raw cracks in the soles of her shoeless feet, the crust of filth around her mouth from hasty eating and no washing. Fights with knives and pieces of glass were commonplace. She has watched as friends chose to die of overdoses. Others died of injuries. Mothers as young as thirteen dying in childbirth with no one caring about their screams. She has lived in that heartless, dark place that the ordinary Athenians deny the existence of, and she has survived.

If this man with his tattered, limp pinky and his scowl and his gun thinks he can bulldoze his way into her life and take anything from her, he has got another think coming. She uncrosses her legs and sprawls out in the heat of the sun whilst taking a good long look over the stern of the boat. In the distance, she can see two boats leaving Saros port. Just dots. But these will grow as they draw nearer. She hopes they will be flying the port police flag.

'What's your name?' Irini asks. Her voice sounds strong. There is no trace of fear, no tremor. The man stops gazing out to sea and looks at her.

'I don't wish to tell you.'

'I am Irini and I need to call you something, as all the way to Casablanca is a long trip, so choose.'

'Call me what you like.' He looks back out to sea. To the east, the sea looks darker, ruffled. The clouds on the horizon are growing puffy and white but the day is getting hotter as the sun climbs to its zenith.

The bakery will be all but empty of bread in the village now. The kafeneio at the top of the square will be open and Theo will be setting out his tables and chairs. The farmers, in baggy trousers and white shirts, sleeves rolled up, waiting at tables set around the dried fountain for him to open, will begin to gather, anticipating his return behind the counter to take his time in brewing their nectar.

Vasso in the kiosk will be watching her portable television, and the doors to Stella's taverna will be thrown open, Mitsos lighting the grill. The small sandwich shop will already have sold out of *bougatsa* after the wave of children passing on their way to wait for the school bus, which is half way in to Saros by now.

She hasn't lived there long, but from working in the shop, she has got to know everyone in the village. During the mornings and the evenings, there is always someone sitting in the shop with her, keeping her company, telling her their tales of woe or sharing their secrets. She has found that she is good at keeping peoples' confidences, and there are plenty to keep. It has given her a sense of belonging. Maybe that is something that she has learnt that could be useful now. Listening, talking, keeping secrets.

The pirate shakes out one leg, pulling his jeans down from the knee.

'Sam,' Irini says.

'What?'

'Your t-shirt says Sam. Capital S, a.m. Like Uncle Sam. Are you American, Sam?'

'I don't want to say.'

With no wind, the day is getting hotter. Sam fidgets in his jeans as if they are sticking to him. He gets up, looks all around the boat at the calm waters, and stares for a while at the two black dots near Saros before dismissing them.

'Don't do anything stupid.' He stands abruptly and with a leap, he is around the helm and descending the steps.

Irini is left alone. She stands. The distance to the shore on either side is too far for her to swim; she is not that good a swimmer. The dots that she hopes are the port police have not grown any bigger but she has no doubt they have powerful binoculars. She has no idea how strong they will be, but it cannot harm to presume they are very strong. With a quick look to the hatch ensuring that Sam is not watching, she waves her arms above her head, but only for a second as a noise from below makes her nervous.

He comes back on deck in a pair of khaki shorts, barefoot and shirtless. He strides over her and back to the helm. Whilst he was down below, the yacht has veered wildly off course and he checks their direction by looking at the land before sitting down again. Irini is staring. There are several dark red, raised scars on his chest, both long and short, and the whole area is pitted with small round welts which she suspects are the result of a shotgun fire, having seen it before after a rabbit hunting accident on Orino Island. Across his stomach, his skin is thin and distorted as if it has melted. In comparison, the smooth brown muscles of his shoulders look unreal. It is only as he lifts his arm to steer that the open wound under his shoulder blade, in that place that is impossible to reach with either hand, is exposed to the air. It is wet with both blood and pus.

'What happened?' She cannot hide the horror in her voice and she gags. Not even on the streets has she seen survivors of anything as brutal as this. She witnessed lots of line scarring and the resulting thin skin of continuous self-harm but, her guess is, these are the remains of some grim wounds that she seriously doubts anyone would, or could, inflict upon themselves.

'Which one?' The tone of his reply kills any further questions, but she cannot stop staring. He tuts and shakes his head, rolling his eyes as if her response is naïve.

Chapter 5

They sit in silence, the motor puttering away, the sound of water bubbling at the bows, churning in their wake. It cannot be much past eight, maybe nine o'clock. It is going to be a long day. The sun is reflecting off the sea so brightly that Irini screws up her eyes to look at the waves. Over by the coast, a small fishing boat moves idly, no doubt trailing a line. A fish for dinner, to be gutted and cooked by his wife, along with *horta*, boiled wild greens the woman has collected herself from the hills behind the cottage that sits by the beach, no doubt.

Just the thought makes Irini's stomach grumble.

The chocolate in the croissant she left on the dashboard in the car will have melted by now, run out of the pastry and puddled in a corner of the wrapper.

Watching the land pass is hypnotising. The rocking of the boat is soothing and it is not long before Irini finds her mind wandering for a few seconds, forgetting where she is and the man who has put her there. When she notices, she sits up straight and tries to keep alert but after some time, her mind wanders again, this time for longer, dreaming of Marina's loan being paid off, the oranges commanding a higher price and being able to afford things for Angelos that she never had as a child. She jolts back into the present and looks at Sam, whose gaze has a more lazy quality to it than before. He has settled in his seat but with his arm at an awkward angle as, with a light touch, he steers the yacht.

'You know that there is an auto-pilot,' Irini says and then wonders why she is saying anything that will make his life easier.

He doesn't even acknowledge her, but continues to sit awkwardly. Presently, he shifts in his seat and tries to steer with his other arm. The position is impossible.

'How does it work?' His eyes meet hers. The dead look has gone and the green of the irises seems lighter. There is something very sad about them.

'Those rubber belts hanging over the steering column.' Irini points. 'They go over the wheel and then over the motor there on the floor and then you turn it on and press auto-pilot.' Until now, Irini would have said that she knows nothing about sailing, but it is amazing how much she must have picked up from Captain Yorgos and his endless tales of personal heroics and the things he has had to do on his boat.

Sam studies the motor on the floor and the simple control panel. Standing, he unloops one of the belts and tries to attach it to the wheel. It looks like he is doing it right, but when the belt is looped over the helm and the motor, there is no tension. Irini has no idea why. Sam studies it for a second and pushes a lever on the body of the motor, tensioning the belt. Turning the control panel on with a flick of a switch, the motor zizzes and turns the wheel, via the belt, just a fraction first one way and then the other until it settles.

Taking his seat again, he mutters a 'thank you' towards her. His right arm lies limply in his lap, his upper arm shadowing his ribs, but the wound beneath his shoulder blade is exposed, open and weeping. The skin around the wetness has jagged edges and in amongst the raw red tissue, there is something yellowish. It is not difficult to guess that without attention, it is not going to close and heal well.

The autopilot motor zizzes again, another tiny correction.

Irini licks her lips. She is thirsty. If there is no water on board, he can hardly be planning to go all the way to Casablanca.

'Can I go below and use the toilet?' She stands. He waves his arm towards the hatch without interest. The autopilot buzzes. The engine putters. For floating at sea, it is very noisy.

Below deck, the engine is even louder, housed as it is behind the steps. The radio is crackling. It would be nice to be in contact with someone out there, to be told again that someone is coming.

'Port police, this is *Artemis*. Come in.' Irini feels nervous about using the radio now that Sam is not stuck at the helm.

'*Artemis*, we hear you. Everything okay? Over.'

She looks up through the hatch. Sam is sitting with his eyes shut. She returns to the radio. 'Yes. Over,' she replies. A long breath escapes through her nose, her free hand rubbing her temples, her chin sinks to her chest.

'We have two boats following you. We will not approach with speed, as we wish to keep the situation as calm as we can. Is everything alright at the moment? Over.'

'Yes. He is calm, but we have no water. Over.' Irini looks towards the hatch. She knows he cannot hear her but still, it feels that talking out loud is a risk and besides, he could come down at any moment. She should never have mentioned the autopilot.

'Rini, Captain Yorgos is here with us. He says there is drinking water under the bunk in the rear guest cabin. Being thirsty may drive him into port, so keep it to yourself if you can.'

'How long does Captain Yorgos think it will be before we run out of fuel? Over.'

Captain Yorgos was happily sitting in the shade of the plane tree, sipping a Greek coffee from a tiny cup when the young port police man in a neatly pressed white shirt ran up to him.

'Captain Yorgos?' the man, really just a boy, addressed him. 'You must come quickly. Your yacht has been taken by a pirate.' After a second's hesitation, Yorgos' laugh roared across the square. Everyone in the café turned to see the source of such a noise but Yorgos did not care. He wanted to share it with everyone, it was such a fine joke. Wondering which one of the port police came up with it, he bet himself that it was Demosthenes, the old rogue. As a commander in the port police, he was all but retired and, as a last request, asked to be stationed in Saros to be at home. Demosthenes was born and brought up here, and his sisters still lived in the old town, not far from the large crumbling family home. Yes, he was the sort of man to have such a sense of humour and the authority to call others into action to carry it out.

'Good one, son. Tell Demosthenes that if he wants me to come over for coffee, all he has to do is ask. But for now, I have a coffee here, so he must come to me.' And he laughed again but the man stood there, looking worried.

'No, sir, really. We have checked him out. He is a known English mercenary. Wanted in three countries. He was detained in Athens yesterday but got away. We suspect he is heading to Libya or Morocco.'

After studying the earnest young man's face, Yorgos stood reluctantly.

'It is an extravagant joke, my friend,' he said. 'But Demosthenes is a good friend, so I will come.

Maybe he has a punch line, eh?' His eyes glinting at the young officer as he threw coins on the table to leave.

The walk hurt. They had to stop several times with the lad urging him on, and he began to believe there really was some emergency. The commotion and noise in the port police office extinguished all thoughts to the contrary.

The petty officer addressed the general hubbub in the room.

'Is Captain Yorgos here yet?' he shouted.

'Here. I'm here.' Captain Yorgos took off his black felt peaked cap. Beads of sweat lined the creases in his brow; blackheads accentuated the depth.

'How much fuel did the *Artemis* have?'

'She was full. Just filled her up last night,' he stammered, mopping his forehead with the hem of his t-shirt.

'Bad news there, I'm afraid. There is a full tank. But we are tailing you, closing in. We are waiting for orders. Over.'

Irini stops rubbing her temples and, with her hand on her hip, looks up and through the narrow window. All there is to see through the window is sky, but the window itself is thick plastic that has been broken down by years of ultra-violet light until it has crazed into a thousand pieces. Sunlight hits the different angles, shimmering into a thousand viewpoints.

'What do you mean waiting for orders? Over.'

'Just that. We might need to make this incident an example. Over.'

'What on earth does that mean?' Irini forgets to let go of the button so there is no reply. Remembering, she releases it.

'It means he will not get away with this. Over.'

'I am more interested in my safety. Over.'

'It would not look good if any harm came to you, Rini. Your safety is paramount. Over.'

Irini is frowning. She mutters to herself, 'It would not look good, not look good?'

She presses the button. 'Who the hell cares how it will look?' Irini finds she is nearly shouting and quickly looks to the blue square of the hatch.

'Stay calm, Rini. Everything that can be done will be done to keep you safe. Over.'

Somehow, the conversation has not surprised her. She hangs up the microphone. The corners of her mouth turn down. 'Not look good!' she mutters to herself as she goes into the toilet. Not much has changed since she lived on the street. The reaction of the police to incidents back then was all about how it looked both to the public and in their records. People were let go who should have been held in custody; others held who should have been released. None of it made any sense and no one seemed to care about the individuals. That's what she had loved so much about the village when she moved there. It was all about people. Each person mattered.

She steadies herself as the boat hits a wave and lurches slightly. With the movement of the boat, things have moved about again in the bathroom. More tubes and bottles from the first aid box are rolling on the duckboard floor. Larger items remain behind the rail fronting the shelf. The first aid box itself is on its side. Rolls of bandages have been pitched into the sink. She grabs the various bottles and tubes and packets of gauze from the floor and the shelf and shoves them into the box.

The disarrayed items do not fit in easily and the lid will not close. Half-open, it will not fit back onto the shelf, and there is nowhere else to put it down flat. Irini uses the toilet with the box on her knee, rinses each hand in turn, holding the box in the other, and goes back out to the salon, where she dumps the box on the table and wipes her hands dry on her jeans.

With a glance to the hatch, she opens the rear cabin door and discovers a six pack of large bottles of water stored under the bunk. She pulls one out and drinks deeply. The water is not cold but to her parched mouth, it is the most wonderful sensation and for a moment, she is lost to everything around her. When she is satiated, she mutters again, 'It will not look good!' and shakes her head at the thought that she is supposed to trust her safety to these people.

On putting the unopened bottles back, she discovers two cartons of orange juice. Her stomach gives her no choice and, tearing one open with her teeth, she drinks again. This time, the sensations of satisfaction are even deeper, resulting in a sigh when she stops to breathe. She will drink the rest later, if the port police have not taken her off before hunger strikes again. The cartons get stuffed back with the water bottles.

The half-drunk water bottle she puts behind the cabin door for easy access.

Back in the saloon, the first aid box, sitting open on the table, seems out of place. Time is one thing she has a lot of at the moment, and she could use it to put everything back in neatly and replace it on the shelf on the bathroom. After giving it a second's thought, the action seems trivial and unimportant. In this present situation, she cares neither for tidiness, or her work, or the port police, or anything belonging to the so-called civilised world.

'It will not look good,' Irini mutters one more time and then mounts the stairs to go on deck, shaking her head at the port police's attitude.

Sam is contorted, trying to see to the wound under his shoulder blade. As he reaches what he can, he winces and sucks air through his teeth. He looks up sharply as she steps out onto the deck and Irini can see his eyes shining, watering. Now ignoring the weeping wound, he looks out at the sea and rests against the chair back as if he has no concerns in the world.

Irini stares at him, finding traces of the man behind the hardened face, but as she looks, his eyes glaze over, the cheek muscle twitches, and he is gone again.

Without premeditative thought, Irini turns around, goes back down into the saloon and comes back up with the bottle of water and the first aid box.

'Here.' She offers him the water. His hand is quick but his mind is in control and he waits for Irini to take it back and drink first. She spins off the cap and takes a sip, and this appears to satisfy him, and he grabs it back greedily and the contents are emptied quickly. When it is gone, he becomes still again.

'Where and why?' he asks.

'Where and why what?' Irini puts the first aid box on the deck and begins to go through the contents.

'Where did you find the water and why did you share it with me? You could have hidden it for yourself.'

Irini shrugs and pulls out two packets of gauze, a bottle of iodine, and a bandage. He watches her, his lips pursed, a slight frown crossing between his eyebrows, his cheek muscle forever twitching.

'Lift your arm.' She squats beside him.

'No. There is no need.' He faces her, the frown growing more intense, looking her in her eyes, searching for her motivation.

'There is a need.' She meets his look, tries again to see the person inside the hard shell. He does not relent and so she sits back opposite him, leaving the gauze and bandages on the teak floor.

'I lived on the streets once.' She says it nonchalantly. His head swivels to look at her briefly before returning his gaze back to the sea.

'My parents died. My *yiayia*, my grandmother that is, she went a bit mad and just left me. The house and land were taken back and I was on the streets.' She says all this watching the waves curling out from the side of the boat, spreading off either side into the distance.

Once, when she was with Petta on the taxi boat he captained for a year on Orino Island, he took her for a ride and dolphins came to play, racing alongside. They stayed with the boat for hours, weaving, jumping, shooting off and then returning to surf on the bow wave. When Petta slowed the boat, Irini ventured to the bow in her bare feet and lay down flat on the deck, looking into the water. The beautiful animal that was just beneath the surface turned onto its side and looked at her, its eye swivelling in its socket to take her all in.

The moment has stayed with her, helped put so much of her life in perspective, separated what is really important from the more trivial. It is difficult to say how it did this, but whenever something comes to her mind, if she weighs it against that moment, it puts everything in a truer perspective.

As she watches the waves now and thinks of Sam and his gun and his bid to get to Casablanca, the port police wanting to make an example of him, she recalls the dolphin turning on its side, looking at her and making contact in that moment. Then a wave broke, churning the sea, and the moment was gone. The dolphin still played in the wake, she still watched it swim, but that intense contact was what she hung onto. That connection.

'It was an unloving, uncaring, environment,' Irini continues. 'There were two types of people on the street. Everyone knew it was dog eat dog. You know that saying?' She does not wait for his acknowledgement. 'We all knew that the only person who would look out for you was yourself. That aside, some chose to strike out at anybody at any time, which I think was from fear, and the others tried to make the immediate world around them a better place, just by acknowledging the other person's position, giving them space, or showing them care if it was appropriate.'

The land on their starboard side is getting further away. Looking to the port side, she is brought up short. Sam is staring at her. She swallows and her eyes widen, adrenaline released. But he does not move and her fear subsides. She understands the emotional shift behind his look though, and slides off her seat, picks up the iodine bottle, and tears open a packet of gauze.

'This will sting,' she says quietly. The autopilot buzzes.

Wiping around the wound shows how jagged the edge are. It is a tear rather than a cut and it's impossible to imagine how it could have happened.

The yellow tinges she saw inside the wound from a distance prove to be fatty tissue. She cannot recognise anything else in the oozing opening, although there are many textures. At least, she consoles herself, it is not down to the rib bones.

Pouring the iodine onto the gauze, she makes quick eye contact before touching it gently to the area and wiping away all that she can. He gulps in air sharply. The fingers of his right hand, all except the limp tattered little digit, take hold of his own tight muscle in his leg and squeeze.

'Sorry,' Irini mutters. His eyes land on her and flash of hatred and the desire to harm. The green irises appear black again and she recoils in fear.

'Pour it on to wash it,' he says through clenched teeth.

Irini wants to ask him if he is sure. If what she has done stung, she cannot imagine how pouring the iodine is going to feel. But to ask him would maybe be to suggest that he does not know his own mind so instead, she picks up the iodine bottle, pours some onto a new piece of gauze and without warning, splashes from the bottle into the wound. He spasms as if he has been shot. A piercing wheezing of air comes from a deep place in his gut, up and out through a tightened muscle in his throat. His face contorts as he explodes with the word 'bugger' which distils across the calm sea around them. He breathes heavily for a few minutes until he takes control, releases his clenched hands, put his chin against his chest, and nods. Irini takes this as her cue to place on the gauze.

He is quite limp as she passes the bandage around his body, across his acid- or fire-burned stomach, over the old scars, around under his other arm and over the defined muscles of his back to pass over the wound again and again, one bandage being attached to the next until the job is done as best she knows how.

She says nothing as she clears away what is left of the gauze and bandage packets. Taking the rubbish below, she puts it in the plastic bag that holds the wet crinkled toilet roll that she put there in what seems to belong to another lifetime. The radio crackles but she ignores it, instead taking on deck the chess set Captain Yorgos keeps in the saloon to challenge his clients in quieter moments.

'Do you play?' she asks as she comes on deck. But Sam's eyes are shut. Lines where tears have washed through dirt trace down his cheeks, and he suddenly looks so young.

Far off behind them, the two dots that must be the port police boats have grown bigger. They really are hanging back! And what did making this 'an example' mean? Usually to use someone as an example means to be overly harsh with them. In Sam's case, what does that mean?

She watches his face. He is younger than Petta, who will be thirty seven this year. But he is older than her, just turned twenty-seven last month. Or maybe he isn't older than her, just more worn. His forehead is smooth and wide, he has no grey hairs. His day's growth of stubble ages him but there are no permanent lines around his eyes, no bagging under them. His lips are smooth.

However old he is, what on earth would drive him to become a mercenary and how on earth is he going to get out of this situation? Being on a yacht in the middle of the sea with port police in speedboats tailing, who only need to push the throttle forward to catch up, he is a sitting duck.

His eyelids flutter.

Chapter 6

As his eyes open, he bucks to his feet. The box of chess pieces is kicked. The pieces spill. A gun appears. His stance is rock solid. He fixes her in his sights, both hands on his weapon.

Open palms towards him, hands either side of her face, eyes wide, she stops breathing. He does not blink.

Slowly he lowers his arms.

Her heart slips from her throat back to its normal place, but it is still beating fast. She wraps her arms around herself, holds everything together, and tries to breathe deeply.

'Did I sleep?' he asks, looking over their wake first at one of the dots that is now close enough to be boat shaped, and then at the other. He does not seemed concerned or surprised to see them.

'Just for a second.' With the beating of her heart returning to normal, Irini bends forward to pick up the chess pieces.

'Do you play?' he asks.

Irini does not answer him. Instead, she pulls out the table that is folded against the helm and sets up the board. He watches.

When she has finished laying them out, the white pieces are on his side but as she takes her hands away, he turns the board so they are nearest her. Frowning, she decides to say nothing and opens. He plays aggressively from the start and within ten moves, she knows she has lost but she plays on anyway. The boat rocks as it moves, the land drifts by on either side, and the sun relentlessly beats down on them as they each take their turns, him taking more time to consider than her.

The first match is over fairly quickly.

'Well, that was a good warm up,' Irini declares and resets the pieces. It is becoming easier to be with Sam even if he is silent. His silence is not tense. Rather, it is tranquil, non-critical.

In the next game, she will think more carefully, take her time, not play so defensively, do something he is not expecting.

She makes the same opening. He makes a different response. She considers.

'I made friends with two boys.' Irini says it casually, testing him to see how he will react to her talking. Sam is leaning his chin into the plan of his hand, elbow on knee. He swaps hands. It gives her the feeling that he is listening.

'Brothers, they were.' She puts her finger on the rook but takes it off again. For years, she has wanted to talk about the things she witnessed on the streets, the things that are outside most peoples' experience. 'We lived in a disused carriage down by the railway lines. The older brother was a few years younger than me, the younger one, so young.' Her finger is back on the rook but she does not play it, just thinks. She takes her finger off again. A few times, she has tried to tell Petta, but Petta could not hear. It distressed him to think she had lived in such a world and those attempts had ended with her comforting him, so she gave up. The images and memories have become locked away deep inside her so although she has continued through her 'normal' life looking like everyone else, she has felt different, not the same as other people, or that she truly belongs. It has always made her feel just a little bit dirty.

'The elder brother went off each day to find food and I did the same. Food and work. The little one stayed and played with the stray dogs. He was too small to walk any great distance.' To Sam, the mercenary, these things she has witnessed may be child's play, daily events for him, no big deal, but it feels so liberating, refreshing even, to be talking about them. If Sam doesn't understand why she is taking the opportunity to talk to someone who has been there too, let it out, exorcise it, he will at least not be shocked. That alone will be a relief. After all these years, she may at least no longer be alone in her horrendous remembered world.

Perhaps playing her castle is a better move. Her finger on the castle again, she twists her lips to one side. He might make the obvious return. She remembers when she returned that time.

'I came back one day and found the elder with the younger in his arms. There was no sound from either of them.' Rubbing her chin as if she weighs up her options on the board, but if she is honest with herself, she is relishing, just a little bit, the telling of the history she is about to share, getting it off her chest, out of her private memories and into the world. After a while she says, 'The little one's leg was missing, a growing black wet patch on the ground.'

Sam does not flinch. Leaning back against the seat gives her a different angle on the chess board, but it doesn't help to know what move to make.

'For a good few minutes, I could not understand what I was looking at. But we lived by a railway line.' She lets the idea sink in so Sam will know what she means without the need to be more descriptive.

'The elder one ever so slowly and gently was rocking the younger one, who lay back in his arms.' Irini remembers wondering where all the people were, why there was no one else there. Why didn't the train driver stop? Maybe didn't see. Maybe he just didn't care.

'The younger one stared at me but as I watched, I saw his disbelief in those eyes of what he was feeling. He didn't seem to be in any pain but minute by silent minute, the black area in the dust grew bigger and the brightness in his eyes dimmed.'

She puts her finger back on the rook and then picks it up, hovers over a potential placement. She squeezes out the tears that tremor on her lower lids, to clear her vision.

'He had never even seen the sea.' Still holding the piece, she looks up and out over the water behind Sam. The boy would curl up in her arms at night. Too young to be without a mother, he had forced her into that role. In the night, he would wake sweating and shivering, his eyes wide, his mouth opened in a soundless scream, clutching her until she rocked him to sleep again. She never found out how they ended up on the streets, but she suspected that rough living was better than what they left. Until that day.

'I watched as the disbelief in his eyes turned to panic and from panic to acceptance and acceptance to peace.'

When she first knelt beside him, he reached for and gripped her fingers like a baby in a pram.

'The light in his eyes grew dull. They no longer seemed to see even though he was still breathing and his chest rose up and down, up and down, smaller and smaller movements until it stopped.' She stretches out her hand as if it is cramping but really, she is trying to rid herself of the sensation of the remembered touch of the boy's fingers growing weaker and weaker until he finally let go.

She places the rook in its new position. 'Neither brother made a sound. It was like we were frozen. Then the elder brother got up and just walked away. I never saw him again. I sat with the child until my legs went numb and then I went for a walk, wondering what I should do with his small body. When I came back, he was gone. There was not much of a trail, but there were paw marks everywhere.'

Sam takes his eyes from the board to look at her. Dolphin eyes are all black; his are definitely green. He stares at her. She lets the seconds pass and then he turns back to the board and considers her move. She has been heard. She is not alone in her experiences. It is a thrilling feeling. It brings a sense of freedom.

His next move is not so aggressive and Irini, although now convinced he is the better player, can see a chance of winning if his playing goes the direction she thinks it might. But it is her turn again and his castle is a threat to her bishop.

Sam looks at the boats following them in the distance.

'Are there binoculars on board?' he asks. Irini has been so absorbed in the game and in her memories, and so used to his silence, that his voice makes her jump.

'Eh, yes. Shall I get them?'

His hand goes to stroke his bandaged side, an indication that it hurts to move. Irini bounds below, grabs the binoculars from a shelf above the chart table, and runs back up the steps on deck. Sam is standing on his seat, facing the boats with his hand open by his side, waiting for the binoculars to be placed in them.

He focuses them. What will she say if he asks why the port police are following them? A game of chess, a confession of experiences does not turn a mercenary into a friend. She closes her eyes. What will she say? But why would he suspect her anyway? Because the only two people who know he is on board are him and her and he hasn't told them. Maybe he will think that someone saw him coming on board. But surely he will be trained, sneaky, able to avoid detection. So it would have to be her. If he thinks she has told them then he'll know the only way it would have been possible is by radio. Surely he would have seen that danger. So why did he keep her below to begin with where she had access to it and has since given her free range to go below whenever she has asked if he knows the radio could be such a threat to him?

'Port police,' he says.

'Really?' She tries to sound surprised. 'Well I suppose, why not? I didn't know they just cruised about, though.'

'They are not cruising about. They are following us,' he says. She cannot hear anything in his voice to tell what he is thinking. There is no anger, no shock, nothing. 'They have been following us since we left Saros.'

Irini feels a sudden heat in her cheeks that subsides as quickly as it rises. It is in sharp contrast to the chill that runs down her back. She swallows.

'Ahhh.' Her tone wavers as if she has just realised something. The truth is she has just thought of an explanation for why the boats are there. 'We didn't go in with our passport numbers.'

'What?' Sam lowers his binoculars and sits back down.

'When you leave port, you are meant to go to the port police with the passport numbers of everyone on board.' This is in fact true and there have been several occasions when Captain Yorgos has sent her to the port police office with a crew list for the next day's outing on her way home, to save him the walk. So lazy.

'Can you radio them in?' he asks. Irini shrugs. She has a feeling the police are meant to actually see the passports and the only reason why Captain Yorgos can go - or she can go on his behalf - with just the numbers is because he has been there so long and the port police know him now so well, they even sit and drink coffee together when work is slack.

Sam turns his attention back to the chess board.

He is a wanted man, the port police are following, and he is serenely considering his next move in chess!

'It's your go,' he says and gnaws on the side of his thumb in concentration.

She looks blankly at the board. Well, what is there for him to do? They are not trying to arrest him. The boat is still motoring along through billowing waves under a blue sky ... The whole situation is all pretty calm, really. Chess does seem like the best option to take their mind off an unknown future. The only option, really. What else would they do?

She opens, a new move.

'Me too,' he says.

'Sorry?'

'I have held a good man whose leg was gone.' He makes his return move. Irini is open-mouthed, the chess game forgotten. She wants to hear of someone else just like her. Find out how he has coped. She is scared that he will not say more. He points at the board, encouraging her move. It is hard to concentrate.

He looks at the dangling flesh on his little finger.

'Did that happen at the same time?'

He says nothing, just stares at the board.

'It's still your go.'

Perhaps it is better that he doesn't say any more. Her own images are enough to cope with. She makes a move but the moment she takes her finger off the piece, she knows it is the wrong move. Besides, witnessing all she has witnessed is not the issue, really. It is how she got to be there in the first place that eats away at her.

Sam makes a counter move and looks at her and narrows his eyes as if to chastise her for her mistake. The sadness she saw earlier is still there, but it is not so evident. He could easily have been one of the people she knew back then.

The next move she makes is defensive. What chance did she have?

'I grew up on a farm. Well, a sort of farm. It was some fields up on the edge of Athens. It would be worth a fortune now. But we only rented it.' With him bent forward over the board like that, she has time to study the top of his head. His hair is short but it grows strongly in two different swirls, a double crown. Is that unusual? They had a goat like that on the farm with a double crown. Sort of. Its fur grew in the normal direction up from its nose until it got to its forehead and then it swirled in the other direction, giving it a little fringe that stuck out.

'Mama and Baba grew vegetables and took them to the *laiki* – the market. Every day, wherever there was one. Some days, they would be up at two in the morning and drive for three hours to sell what they could and then drive home, tend the fields, and go to bed to do it all again the next day.'

Marina, back in the village, grows vegetables. In the courtyard, she grows winter lettuces and tomatoes along the wall and out in their nearest orange orchard, she has cleared a space and has planted carrots and onions, herbs and squashes. Now that they live there too, Petta has planted potatoes, which Marina has avoided in the past because they are too hard for her to dig, and cheap enough at the market.

She sighs. A coffee in the courtyard, Angelos playing with… She stops herself. Thoughts like that serve no purpose.

Sam still hasn't taken his turn. He looks back at the port police boats. She wants to distract him from thinking about them.

'So from when I was a baby, they left my yiayia, my grandmother, in charge.' She sighs again but with this sigh, her mouth draws into a straight line. 'You know what I can remember, and people have told me it is not possible, that our memories don't go that far back, but mine does. I remember my yiayia passing me when I was still young enough to be in a cot. You know the sort, with bars all the way around.'

Sam watches her face as she talks. He will not be shocked, he will not need comforting.

'I didn't like the cot because when everything was quiet, sometimes the rats would come out through the holes in the corners and from behind the few bits of furniture we had, sniffing hopefully, their claws tapping tiny sounds as they ran from place to place looking for scraps. Looking down on them from my cage, I found them frightening but I felt safe because I was high up. It was the sound of their claws on the wood. That scuttling, clicking noise. But if an adult was there, they didn't come out, and there was usually an adult there. But this is not really the point. I was telling you about Yiayia.

'Sometimes Yiayia would mother me as if I was the most precious thing in the world to her. Caring and kind.' She smiles at this memory and then the smile drops. 'The next moment, it was as if I did not exist. The change was so sudden, as if something had shifted in her head, in her thinking. Even if I cried at those times, it was as if she could not hear me. Her eyes glazed over and often, she would rock and stare out of the window and I would be frightened of her. Other times, it was even worse, as if I was something evil and dirty. If I cried for long enough at these times, she would throw the end of a piece of bread in my cot with me and then go out to the fields. During the course of the day, she would come in and out but each time, it was as if she was searching for something and she never seemed to see me.' Irini stops talking to see if Sam will encourage her to continue.

With a glance, he does. She prepares herself before she continues. 'But, and this is the bit that no one believes. I remember getting hungry and looking amongst the crumpled covers for the piece of bread and finding a rat with its teeth sunk into it. It showed no fear, this rat. I grabbed the bread and pulled and only then did it jump from my cot. After that, being alone was frightening. I thought the rats were going to eat me.'

Sam's expression does not change. But nor does he show any signs of disbelief. Nor does he laugh, which someone did once. He just listens and Irini feels a great relief. She allows the feeling to settle within her before saying more. But eventually she feels driven to go on.

'But although the rats were the immediate problem, it was my yiayia that caused the hurt. I never knew what mood she was going to be in, and what I did didn't seem to influence her moods. It was all so uncertain and I craved her love, you know?' She has never admitted this even to herself before. 'Mama and Baba where there for so few hours a day, and when they were, they were either in the fields or sleeping. Yiayia was more like a mother to me because she was there the most. But trying to explain what it was like growing up with her. Well, it's difficult to explain without sounding bad.'

'You have told this to your husband though?' he says, looking at her wedding ring.

The mental image of Petta fills her with love and yearning but also a loneliness. She cannot share this part of her life. He cannot even listen to it.

'He finds it too hard to think of me in these situations.' It is uncomfortable to confess this and she senses she is being disloyal. She waits for Sam's judgement on Petta, but he says nothing.

Picking up the binoculars, he takes another look at the port police.

'They will wait until it is dark,' he says.

Chapter 7

'Wait for what?' Irini asks, but he does not answer.

The clouds over the horizon have grown mountainous; where they meet the horizon, they are dark and foreboding. The sea in that direction is green and ruffled, not enough for white caps to form but not the smooth silk of transparent blue that surrounds them. The gentlest of breezes lifts the longer strands of her cropped hair.

An image of Stathoula comes to mind. Her plane will have landed now, and she will be in the car, on her way down from the airport. Irini pushes the thought away, but at the same time is interested to note that the intensity with which she was anticipating Stathoula's visit has diminished a little.

'Put the sails up,' Sam says. Irini looks at him blankly. 'You know how?' he asks. In theory, she knows how, sort of. She could take the cover off the boom and undo the mainsail. She could probably figure which ropes to pull to get it aloft but then? She has seen tourists leaving harbour with the mainsail flapping pointlessly, more of a hindrance than an aid. She doubts she would be able to do any better.

'You have no idea, do you?' Sam asks. He looks at the port police boats behind them. They are getting no closer. 'I don't suppose we could outrun them anyway, even if there was a strong wind and we knew what we were doing.'

Irini wonders at what point he began to see them as a *we*. She suspects it is a positive sign as far as her safety is concerned. With that thought, she wonders if she had better check in with the port police, find out what is happening. Surely it is just a matter of coming alongside and telling him that he is under arrest. Would he be stupid enough to use his weapon against them? There are two boats and no doubt half a dozen officers on each - all armed, presumably.

She looks at Sam. He is in a bad position, a sitting duck. Why have the police not come already?

'So, with two parents and a grandmother, how did you end up on the streets? Did you run away?' He seems to have lost interest in the chess. He leans back and stretches his arms out on either side of him, along where the cockpit seat moulds with the upper decking. His head rocks back and he closes his eyes.

'It was black and white growing up,' Irini begins. 'My parents loved me, adored me even.' A smile crosses her face and she sinks, just a little, into her seat. 'Sometimes, if they came home late, they would wake me just to see me, which I would love.'

Irini stretches out, mirroring his position but she keeps her eyes open, watching his face. Talking to him has taken such a weight from her, the least she can do is entertain him with a tale, a bit of her history, to keep his mind from the port police.

'But Yiayia treated me like I was a problem. It got to the point as I grew that if I agreed with everything she said, then she was bearable, but I felt like I was living a lie to agree with some of her views. If I disagreed with her, it was as if I had unleashed a dragon.' The simile amuses her and she laughs in the back of her throat, briefly. Sam still has his eye closed but he actually smiles. The creases on either side of his mouth are exaggerated and dimples form.

'But one day, they did not come home. I went to bed and in my dreams I waited for them to wake me, but they didn't. The next day after school, I rushed back to the farm expecting to see Mama bent from her hips weeding, Baba lifting and digging. But the field was empty.'

She stops talking. The emotions are still too fresh even though it was over twenty years ago. Yiayia didn't need to tell her. She knew something had happened and the world she looked out on stretched away, seeming impossibly big and very, very lonely.

'Irini,' her yiayia called. She never did call her Rini, always Irini, as if being slightly formal would keep her at a distance. It did.

'Come in,' the old woman commanded. But Irini could not see the point of moving. There was no van in the drive. There was no Mama or Baba to love her. She stood in the drive unmoving and ever so slowly, she began to tremble. It started with her legs, up into her stomach, which quivered and knotted, seeped up into her chest, strangling her breath as it rose to her throat. Her mouth wobbled, her bottom lip quivered, and her vision blurred, swimming in unspilt tears.

'Come in, do you hear me?' Yiayia shouted, but her legs no longer seemed to be part of her and so she didn't move. It took her yiayia's hand on the back of her neck, gripping and pushing her, to make her walk into the house.

'Where are they?' she asked, once out of the glare of the late afternoon sun, but she knew the answer.

Yiayia just looked around the room, her eyes so wide, as if surprised. Then she began to lay the table for four people and talked to Irini as if she was her mama, asking her about her next trip to market, and how the last one went. Then Yiayia started asking Irini where Irini was and what time would she be home from school, complaining that the food would burn, even though none was cooking. So Irini shook her. Yiayia's eyes rolled in her head and then she refocused and saw her grandchild and her mouth went small and tight and she walked out of the house.

Irini calms herself before she continues. She feels a little dizzy.

'I just sat at the empty table. I knew but I also needed to know. So when she came back in about half an hour later, I asked her where Mama and Baba were and she said that it would be just me and her now.' Irini's eyes rest on the sea. The images are as clear as if it were happening right now.

'What do you mean?' She heard her own words, the squeal of the sound that was her voice, but she refused to let any tears fall in front of Yiayia.

'A car accident. Fatal.' That was it. That was all Yiayia said. This was her son they were talking about, and that was all she said. 'Now you can start by making a salad,' Yiayia commanded. Irini turned away from her and looked at the wilted, unwashed vegetables on the table that Mama had brought in the day before.

This house that she grew up in was no more than a few storage rooms that her mother had whitewashed and tried to make home with curtains that were too lean in fabric to close on the inside. Outside, with empty cans and old, split buckets filled with soil and planted with flowers, she had created the illusion of domesticity. Irini's enduring image is of her mother toiling every day without rest, before she got up and after she went to bed. The sun beating down upon her bent back, her face the colour of a chestnut as she stood, dry and creased into a smile. As Irini grew older and her school days got longer, there was less time spent at home with only Yiayia, and life seemed easier for it.

There had also been an added element of excitement coming home from school, as Mama would be back from whichever market they had been to. She would be in the fields and when Irini came walking up the track, she would call her to come over and once close enough, wrap her in a hug and cover her head with kisses. She smelt of soil. Mama would ask her what she had learned that day and as Irini talked, she continued her work, her face glowing with pride.

Wet soil smelt best, after the rain. But the smell of dry, dusty soil was also good when mixed with the faint traces of Mama's sweat and her own unique personal odour.

The day Irini learnt of her mother's death, the soil was wet.

'Salad,' Yiayia commanded. But as she said it, a car drove up the track and came to a halt. It was one of the other stall holders, come to offer his respects. Then another car and another, and slowly the house began to fill with strangers. The level of talking grew as new people came in. Arrangements were being made; a funeral director arrived. With stiff limbs, Irini walked out of the storage room that they used as the kitchen and into the next room, which was her parents' bedroom. From a nail in the wall, she unhooked her mama's housecoat that she used to protect her clothes as best she could when she worked in the field. Slipping her arms through the sleeves, it engulfed her, but she pulled it tightly around her waist and fashioned a belt from some green twine.

'What on earth do you think you are doing?' Yiayia thundered. She hadn't noticed her come in.

'If they are dead, who will till the soil, grow the vegetables, go to the *laiki* to make the money to pay the rent?' Irini asked, her voice quiet, everything on hold, nothing showing, nothing leaking, closed up.

Yiayia was not able to answer.

Within six months, most of the crops had failed. It was too much work for one person and Yiayia's eyes grew more vacant and she took to wandering off, so much of Irini's day was spent finding her and bringing her back.

The other problem she faced was how to get the produce to the markets. The traders who had shown so much sympathy initially were kind enough to come to her to buy what she had. But their compassion seemed to melt away when it came to haggling about the price. Before the year was out, the rent was so much in arrears that they were given notice.

The day the owner came to tell them that they needed to think about finding alternative accommodations, a strange look passed over Yiayia's face. Once the landlord was gone, she suggested that Irini go to bed early and after years of habitual conforming, she complied. When she woke the next day, Yiayia's coat and handbag where gone. There was no sign of the old lady either.

Sam opens his eyes as she finishes her story. With his head tipped back, he was looking through them half-closed. Crossing her hands across her chest does nothing to make her feel less exposed. What could he say to make what happened to her feel any better? She is now not sure why she has laid herself so open.

Unsure what to do, she does nothing. He continues to look at her through slitted eyes. His lips twitch. He is going to speak.

'They loved you.' His voice is soft and he says it like it is something so special, so precious, everything else should be eclipsed by this fact. Irini cannot meet his eye, but her arms drop from across her chest and she has a strange sensation of safety. Her breathing, which was shallow, now becomes even and deep. The sea's blue around them seems to have lightened. The slight wind is creating more movement on the surface, which increases the sparkle.

'Do you have family?' she asks. But the openness that was there the moment before closes. His eyes are still green but they look only out. There is no invitation in. His mouth is a thin line.

Chapter 8

Captain Yorgos stands in the middle of the room. The port police station is on the first floor over a taverna in one of the grand old houses that face the harbour. The floor is of worn unpolished parquet. The shutters are all thrown open on three sides of the large room, giving a magnificent panoramic view of the bay. The floor space has been divided up into offices with pine partitions which have framed windows above waist height. The plaster walls at the back of the room crumble with age and the solid wooden desks, Yorgos happens to notice, all have folded cardboard wedges under one leg, presumably to stop their rocking on the time-warped floor.

Young men in white short-sleeved shirts are rushing about with a nervous energy that makes him dizzy, and he looks around for a seat.

'Ah Yorgos. No good, no good.' Commander Demosthenes puts a hand on his shoulder and shakes his hand. 'Come, let's go into my office.' With his hand remaining on Yorgos' shoulder, he leads the way to a cubicle in the far corner that is slightly bigger than the rest. The sun streams through the open windows and casts stripy shadows through a shutter that has blown closed. The head of the port police indicates a seat for Yorgos and pushes the shutter open again. Some insect with dangling legs flies in through one window and out through another. Commander Demosthenes sits in the chair behind his desk and swivels to face Yorgos.

'Right, so who is on board? We have been in touch with an Irini. Is there anyone else?' Yorgos has never seen Demosthenes anything but jovial over coffee. This serious man in front of him is a stranger but as he speaks, the reality that his yacht has been taken begins to sink in, along with the ramifications.

'Do you think my insurance will cover this?' Yorgos asks.

'No idea. Let's see if we can get it back in one piece, shall we? Who is this Irini, and who else could be on board?'

The yacht captain stares out through the open window across the bay. He had six Swiss tourists lined up for today and they have already paid a deposit. Will he have to pay that back?

'No chance of getting her back by ten, then?' he asks with a grin, but his stomach has sunk inside him. Without *Artemis*, it will be a hard season and even harder winter trying to survive and make the remaining yacht seaworthy for the following year with only half his income.

The port police commander looks back blankly.

'Irini is from the village. She arrived alone this morning, but some days in the past, she has come with her little boy. She cleans the boats.'

'Okay. You know her surname?'

'No. But she is married to Marina's son. Marina with the corner shop.'

Demosthenes does not pause to thank him. Without a word, he is on his feet and out of the office, shouting for people to find Marina and her son. 'Find out if the child is at home or on the boat.' Someone retorts that Marina's son is Petta and that Marina's eldest daughter is Eleni and she is in the port police on Orino Island. Someone replies, 'One of ours,' and the activity and the noise seem to grow.

Captain Yorgos puts a hand to his pocket for his cigarettes but finds he must have left his lighter with his coffee in the square. This Irini, he hopes she will keep his boat safe. He should have stayed, at least with him there, the outcome would not be at the whim of some pirate. He would have stood up to him. No doubt this woman is cowering in one of the cabins crying whilst his yacht is being sailed away to, well, to where exactly?

'I've got Petta the husband on line two, Captain,' calls a young man in a white shirt. Yorgos begins to stand but on seeing Demosthenes' broad-shouldered body cross the room, he sits again. It is the other captain they want. He looks at his oil-stained hands, his split nails and then straightens his sagging t-shirt over his rounded belly.

'Well, I am very glad your son is with you. Yes, yes, we will do everything we can to keep Irini safe.' There is a pause. Demosthenes looks through the partition glass and offers a thumbs up. Yorgos manages a smile. Six clients. It is not often he gets six in one day, each paying the day rate. He will lose it all. Six of them.

'Well that's good at least.' Demosthenes shuts the door behind him to keep the noise out. 'The child is at home. But I think they are all coming here. They do that, you know, on the rare occasions that a boat is lost or there's a storm. No matter how much we tell them that there is nothing they can do but wait, they want to be here, as if that will make a difference.' He lights a cigarette and offers Yorgos one. Yorgos notices that Demosthenes' hands are clean and his nails manicured.

'Well, I suppose the same applies to me,' Yorgos declares and stands. His legs hurt every time the blood moves through them. Standing is as bad as walking sometimes.

'No, no, it is good to have you here. Sit down and I will get someone to make you a coffee.'

The coffee takes its time but it arrives before Irini's family. Yorgos knows them immediately from their worried faces. The man is tall and broad and his face looks like it is unused to frowning, the laugher lines around his eyes indented more than the lines on his forehead. These villagers have it easy: just sit around and the oranges grow themselves. Even sends his wife out to work, so what sort of man is he?

The woman behind him, now she looks like she has worked all her life. The sort of woman who wears black for years but this woman has on a blue dress. Unusual. Her footwear is predictable: shapeless black lace ups.

The child in her arms looks like the man.

There is a general gathering of people around them. Soothing noises to the child and woman and low tones to the man. The family begin a barrage of questions: who else is on board, do they know who the pirate is, what are they going to do about it, when will they act? Demosthenes answers as best he can, tries to comfort them but, it seems, he does not lie. Their questions go on and on until they run out of steam and they deflate.

Captain Yorgos looks away, out of the window, as Demosthenes leads the family of three to his office. He should go. Make his excuses and leave.

'Captain Yorgos, this is Petta, Marina, and little Angelos.' The commander ruffles the sleepy child's head. 'Do you people want some coffee? It will be a long wait, I am afraid. The powers that be have taken an interest, which often delays action. But please,' his hand extends and rests gently on the woman's shoulder, 'that is only a good thing.' No one seems to want coffee and the commander leaves them alone.

'I was just leaving, actually.' Yorgos screws up his eyes in anticipation of the pain as he takes hold of the chair's armrests to lever himself up.

'Please Captain Yorgos, do you know anything more that we haven't been told? Do you know this man that has taken Irini? Has this sort of thing ever happened before?' The woman in blue puts her hand on his arm. The child wriggles from her grasp and goes to his baba.

The woman, what was her name? Marina, that's it. She has a kind face and eyes, which look as if they could dance with joy under different circumstances. Good figure too, strong legs.

'How will she sit still? She has so much energy, she likes to be doing something all the time.' Petta begins talking about Irini but his voice quivers and fades, the tears in his eyes spill over, and he picks up his boy and hugs him, burying his own face in the child's hair.

A silence pervades the room. Marina and her son become as statues; even the boy is still. It feels difficult to stand up and walk out, so Captain Yorgos continues to sit where he is, wiggling his toes to keep some circulation going.

Chapter 9

'Oh my goodness, what's that?' Irini points to the sea behind Sam. He turns, winces, puts his hand to his side and then swivels on his seat. The flat water is broken into a thousand white caps, each reflecting a piece of the sun. It takes a moment to even see the fish.

'Flying fish!' Irini's voice is high-pitched.

Sam stands to get a better look, only to step back into Irini, who puts her hands on his hips to stop him falling back onto her. Staring at the winged creatures, neither of them move, dazzled by the light reflecting colours off the breaks in the water and the wings of the fish.

Thlap. Sam's head turns to look towards the bow. A fish has misjudged and lays flapping and gawping on the deck under the boom. *Thlap.* Another one by the cockpit, its tail wiggling from side to side in a frantic attempt to become airborne again.

'Oh, Poor things.' Irini grabs the one in the cockpit and tries to throw it overboard but the fins open again, the tail thrashes, and it slithers back onto the deck.

Sam's hand on her shoulder jerks her back as she goes to grab the fish again.

'What?' she demands.

His face is so close to her, she can see the individual hairs of his beard just emerging through his skin, the open pores around his nose, which eyelashes are stuck together, the pattern in his irises. She can hear the rhythm of his breathing.

Another fish lands.

Irini blinks and he's no longer close. He is rooting in his bag by the helm. Something flashes a reflection in the sun. His actions are all swift, nominal, without warning. One stride takes him back to her, a knife pointing to her stomach.

'Why?' she squeals and backs out of the cockpit and under the boom. Continuing his course, he doesn't even acknowledge her and with a stab and a pull, the fish wiggles wildly and then lies still.

Her mouth is open. It is not that she has not seen a fish killed before, but it is the minimalism of his movements that shocks. Already he is on the other fish by the boom and then one on the side deck, throwing each fish back into the cockpit as he progresses.

The flapping and the skimming of the fish in the water around the boat stops and after the rush of movement, everything seems very still.

'You can cook?' Sam asks.

'If there's oil, we can fry them.' Irini realises she just called them *we*!

'Dry cook them if there isn't.' He swiftly cuts off a fin and studies it as he splays it out into a wing before throwing it overboard, and the rest of the fins follow in quick succession along with their guts. His dexterity surpasses that of any fisherman she has watched and she wonders about his origins. The four fish lay in the cockpit amongst blood and scales. The deck is dotted with patches of blood.

As she fries, she can hear the radio hiss. The ridiculousness of her situation occurs to her - she is frying fish for a pirate on a boat she cannot sail, waiting to be rescued! Could life be any more uncertain, unpredictable? Petta will be wondering where she is by now. Oh *Panagia*, what if he goes down to the port and sees that the boat is gone? What will he think? He will be beside himself, frantic. Maybe she should contact the port police and tell them to let him know that she's alright. Just bobbing along, frying fish!

The fish is beginning to brown. She turns it over, sprinkles on a little oregano that she finds in a cupboard.

But the thoughts of Petta will not go. Her chest tightens and she stabs at the fish with her spatula. She has a steady, stable life full of love and proper beds and a place she can call home and, if Petta isn't enough of a blessing, she has a child. So precious. Her whole life is so incredibly precious and all thrown into jeopardy just by being in the wrong place at the wrong time. From that point of view, life was a lot easier when she had nothing. When she had nothing, there was nothing to lose.

Stathoula – how kind it was of her – took her in straight from the funeral, no questions asked, gave her a bed with springs and sheets. That smell of clean was blissful, and even today she uses the same washing powder Stathoula used then to remind her of that day. She gave her three meals a day, stability, love, and clean sheets. Stathoula gave life value; she gave her value, and that brought Petta.

To find love was to grow strong, stronger than she ever imagined she could feel. With Petta, she can do anything. But to find that love is also to know fear. Not the fear of Yiayia losing her temper and bringing out the wooden spoon, or the fear of some angry guy on the street wanting money or food or something more. That was all just physical, momentary. No, to know love has also brought the fear of losing that love. An unimaginable loss that drains away hope, and beyond that, there is nothing but darkness and despair. It is always hope that dies first.

The fish are almost burnt. She snatches them from the stove.

'*Agamo...*' She leaves the end of the swear word unfinished. Scraping the skin off gets rid of most of the burnt bits and once slid onto a plate, they look presentable. From the cabin at the front, she takes another water bottle but realises she will have to confess to the whole stash if she takes another on deck. It was a six pack. They have drunk one. She will take another up and leave three in plain view, pretend there were only five in the first place.

She puts the fish at the top of the steps along with plates and forks. She follows with glasses and the water.

'I found a whole stash,' she confesses. 'We have three more after this.' There's that *we* again. As they are both in the same boat, it might as well be a *we*, she supposes.

Sam is dividing the fish. Irini has never really been a big fan of fish but she is hungry and makes quick work of her first fish, gulping water down as she eats. Sam eats really slowly.

'Is it too burnt to eat?' she asks.

Sam is in his own world and seems to come out of a daze to answer her.

'No. But our saliva begins the breaking down process. We get more from our food the more we chew. It breaks down the simple sugars and it is the first stage of fat digestion, as it causes us to secrete an enzyme from the gland beneath our tongues.' He takes another mouthful, chewing slowly, and his face becomes blank again. Only when all his fish is gone, which is sometime after Irini's plate is clean, does he drink.

On his second glass of water, he looks behind them. The port police have gained on them slightly but have widened out so they are trailing behind on either side.

'Can you swim?' Sam asks.

'Yes, well, a bit.'

'So why don't you jump? They would pick you up.'

'I didn't think I had that choice.'

'What is to stop you?'

'Well, you.' The plate, unattended on her knee, begins to slip to the floor. He puts his hand out to save it.

'Thank you.' But it is a mutter more than a reply. She is trying to reassess the situation. Is he serious? Would he let her go?

He is watching her face and smiling, but it is a private smile. Is he laughing at her?

If he says she can go, does she jump and risk that he means it? Or maybe it's a plan so he can shoot her in the water, which would take at least one of the police boats off his trail, especially if he shot just to wound. The journey back to the hospital would be paramount. That would give him only one police boat to deal with.

She looks at the coastline on either side of them. If she is correct in her judgement, then they are more than halfway to where the land to the left falls away and the sea channel opens that leads to Orino Island. At the next headland is a good-sized town with their own port police. They could send another police boat from there fairly quickly.

'You know there is a town not far down that coast?' She points. 'They could send another port police boat from there. It would not take long to get here.'

He doesn't even bother looking where she is pointing. Nothing seems to register of what she has said. Maybe it is not a plan to get rid of one of the boats.

So she could jump.

She stands. She actually feels rather bloated and full after the fish, and the last thing she feels like doing is swimming. But standing is a statement. She will have to follow it through.

Did she bring anything on board that she needs to take with her? Her arrival this morning seems so long ago, it is hard to remember. Her phone is in her car, along with her croissant. The thought of the croissant after the fish makes her feel a bit queasy and she wishes she hadn't eaten so fast.

'You need to change course in an hour or two if you are going to Orino Island to pick up fuel and water,' she suggests, but she knows he is not and she is just buying time before she jumps.

'Now why would I go to Orino Island and make it easy for the port police when the fuel gauge says full and you have found drinking water?' Sam's eyes stare again, green iris back to shark's black.

'How do I know you will not shoot me if I jump?' Irini asks. His jaw muscle is twitching again, his face hard.

His answer is a shrug.

'Is that it? A shrug?' Irini's voice raises.

He shrugs again.

'Oh come on. My life is only worth a shrug?' Her voice raises. How dare he dismiss her life so

101

effortlessly? 'You kidnapped me, forced me to be here against my will, and the best you can do is shrug?' She is shouting. Damn him, he will react, her life is worth some reaction, any reaction. She won't be depreciated to being valueless; she is not on the streets anymore. 'You have me in fear of my life and you don't even feel that you owe me an answer if I ask if you are going to shoot me?' Her hands are on her hips and she has taken a step towards the stern of the boat. He looks puzzled but he stays seated.

'What kind of coward are you?' She takes another step around the helm and is onto the bathing platform at the rear of the boat. He has still not moved, making no attempt to stop her. There is no sign of his gun. With her hands clasped together, she points them over her head and bends her knees. The water churns with the motor, a froth of white foam. 'Better get your gun,' she spits, bending her knees even more, her thigh muscle tensed, ready to dive. She will, she will dive, she would rather dive and be shot than …

'I was four when I told my Dad I didn't love my aunt.'

'What?' Irini looks back. Her legs straighten.

'He said she was ill and we need to go and see her.'

Irini lowers her arms.

'I said I did not want to go. I didn't like my aunt.'

As he speaks, she turns back to face him.

'He said, "What are you talking about, of course you love your aunt. She is a good woman." But what I felt was not love, and he told me that it was. It confused me.' Sam's chin sinks a little. His eyes are on his ragged little finger. With the finger of his left hand, he plays with the flap, flicking it backwards and forwards. Holding onto the helm, Irini listens to him.

'That was the first time that I really remember, but it felt familiar so it must have happened before.' He stops flicking his little finger. 'You see…' He sits up, looks her in the eyes. She lets go of the helm and takes a step towards him. 'The child refuses to give up on believing that it can win the love of its parent.' He sounds like a textbook and Irini thinks she can see in his eyes all the lonely hours he must have spent reading to make sense of this four-year-old's memory. She sits opposite him, mirroring, his forearms resting on his knee, his body bent forward, but her head is lifted, watching him, gazing intently.

'Despite abundant evidence to the contrary,' he concludes, but Irini is not sure if this is textbook or personal. Either way, he is back in control and she is still on board.

Did he allow himself to become vulnerable to stop her jumping in, leaving him, losing his bargaining position – if he needs one – with the port police? Or even losing his human shield. She sits back and looks out to the stern. The port police are still a long way away but it would not take long for them to reach her. It was a cheap trick to keep her on board, but it has only delayed her going. She stands.

'You said you had this with your grandmother,' Sam says, 'This pressure to conform to expectations. A pressure that is so relentless and uniform that you are hardly aware of it.'

No one, not even dear sensitive Petta, has ever talked to her enough to understand what it was like living with Yiayia and now, here is this man, who she has only known for a few hours, speaking words as if he lived by her side all her life.

He continues. 'They say that if you put a frog in a pan of cold water and put it on the stove and heat the water slowly, it will not jump out. There is no given point when the frog can decide the water is hot enough. One degree is bearable, the next is so close so that is bearable too; how does it know when to jump?'

'Is that true?' She turns back to him. He sort of nods, the corners of his mouth turned down as if to say *I think so*.

'With Yiayia, I always felt so unreal,' Irini says and Sam nods as if say it was the same for him, he understands. 'If I did well at school, it was great telling Mama but when it was brought to the attention of Yiayia, I felt like a fake, that the success was just gold over dirt. So if I succeeded, it was just a cover up and if I failed, that was the truth. I was dirt, something to be trodden into the ground with all the other dirt until I was nothing, until I didn't exist. Failure or success: Either way, there was no point to my existence.' Irini stops and draws breath. 'Does that sound like madness?'

She sits again. The fish is still sitting there undigested, a weight holding her down.

'I understand.' Sam makes eye contact. 'When I tried to become independent, my father treated it like a betrayal,' he says. 'The reality is that we accept whatever we are fed because, as children, we have to presume good intentions since the alternative is too frightening to consider. He was so proper, I presumed his way was the way, the only way.'

The sun has done nothing but grow hotter as the day has progressed, but a shiver runs the length of Irini's spine. She sits with her legs together, her arms clamped to her sides, her hands interlocked on her knees, and her head bowed. The fish blood on the teak decking is dry now, the scales stuck.

'I was crying one day as a boy,' Sam offers. The tension in Irini's locked fingers lessens as he speaks. 'I can't remember what for. He would cuff me, you know, like this with the back of his hand.' Sam demonstrates throwing the back of his hand across open air. 'The cuffs were a normal part of the day. A hit for not washing up properly, for my shirt hanging out, for not having good manners at the dinner table, for not, oh you understand, for whatever he wanted it to be for.' Sam feels so close. She does not raise her head but she looks up at him, blinking her wet lashes.

'This day he saw me crying, I was about five, and I could tell by the look on his face he did not like hearing me cry. Maybe he felt guilty? Maybe he did not like the show of weakness because it reminded him of his own weakness. I do not know.' Sam stays leaning towards her until the distance between them is only a hand width. 'He said...' Sam falters and begins again, 'He said "Sam..."'

Irini looks up briefly at his use of the name she has given him, and is surprised to find that it saddens her that he chose not to use his real name.

'"Sam, I want you to stop crying now," is what he said. "Stop crying immediately." It seemed like a very hard and cruel thing to ask.' Sam sniffs dryly. 'There was no concern for why I was crying but only this command to immediately stop, just to please him.' He looks past her ear, out to the sea beyond. 'It was so abrupt, uncaring, and I was still spinning, inside my head, trying to understand, make sense of it all when he said, "I want you to laugh." I can remember the feeling of my wide eyes and my mouth hanging open, the air I was breathing cold as I drew it in past my teeth. He always had the windows open and it was winter.' He gives a short gruff laugh. 'At the time, I could not understand what he was saying or why he was saying it. "Laugh, laugh now," he commanded and so I tried to laugh. You see, I wanted his love, I wanted to please him and I forced my tears to be laughter.'

They face each other, Irini seeing the reflection of herself in his eyes. 'I surrendered myself that day, Rini,' he says. It is the first time he has used her name, and it is soft. 'I surrendered my sense of

106

self in order to win his approval. Five years old and I was lost.'

She is not sure if he moves or if she does, but her little finger touches the limp flesh of his little finger, his hands clasped together. He does not pull away and she stretches out her little finger without unlocking her hands and delicately strokes his knuckles. It soothes her, comforting the child he was, not the man, in the way she once wished to be comforted. Her shoulders drop slightly and the tension around her mouth relaxes, giving a fullness to her lips.

'After that, I felt nothing. I just went through the motions; something was broken. He did the same sort of thing again and again, challenging me to surrender, but it was no challenge. I just did as he asked every time.' He sighs and sits back, breaking contact.

'He was in the army.' His voice is brisk again, back in control. 'He went away on manoeuvres and I was left behind. No mother. She was long gone. Sometimes absent in body but always absent in spirit, eh? Then there was this one manoeuvre.'

The silence that follows is so long, Irini is about to ask if he came back.

'Then his unit was rumoured to be returning and I was so excited, because a boy never stops needing the love of his father, no matter what.' He seems to be quoting something he has read again, but there is a sarcastic edge to his voice.

'I went to where the trucks were rolling in and other children were there too, jumping up and down, thrilled. We were looking into the trucks trying to see our fathers. Mothers were trying to stop their children running up before the trucks stopped. To stop any accidents, it was arranged that they drove into a cordoned-off area where we were not allowed to go. Here, they all disembarked and then walked out toward their families. When I saw my father I ran to him with my arms open, ready to hold him.' Sam sucks his bottom lip into his mouth and slowly releases it, his whole jaw and neck in tension. 'He would not embrace me.'

He pauses and lifts each shoulder up in turn as he rolls his head on his shoulders, unknotting his tension. 'I thought at first it was because he was shy, so I watched all the other children with the fathers embracing and giving kisses as I followed my father to our room. I thought once we were there, in private, he would show me some affection. But even with the door closed, he would not come near me and I felt like I was nothing. I mean, if he would not love me then who would?' He pauses for breath.

He asks his question as he leans forward again, reducing the distance between them so their fingers touch again. His eyes are red-rimmed, but they are dry.

Chapter 10

'He sent me to an all-boys military boarding school after that.' His face turns ashen and his limbs seize. His pupils grow wide and dart about although he is still. His stomach is visibly turning. Irini pulls her feet towards her, worried that he is going to be sick; he seems to have trouble swallowing. A little colour returns to his cheeks, his shoulders drop a little and, as if he has got past something impassable, he continues on with what, at first, sounds like relief. 'Then one day in the holidays, I was at the base with him. I was maybe twelve, thirteen. I was outside playing with some other children. One of them was being unkind to me, so I moved away from them, I tried to play somewhere else. But the unkind one, he followed me and made some more derogatory remarks. The other children followed him, stood behind him to see what was going to happen, and his words became more cruel.'

Sam takes her hand. Irini can see them, on a bare concrete lot in an army camp, nothing to play with and without anything to do until an ugly big boy starts picking on the sensitive child with the green eyes and then everyone is suddenly entertained. Everyone except the boy with the green eyes.

'I felt like a bubble had closed around me. I was looking out into a world that was not real and I had this thought as he spoke to me, a thought about all the heroes in the films I had watched alone in the house when my father was out. Heroes who, when they got picked on, punched the other person and everyone cheered. Still in my bubble, I can remember thinking that I had never hit anyone and I wondered what it would feel like to be my father, the aggressor.' He has both her hands now, stroking them, soothing his own words.

'So I turned on him and I told the boy to stop and he laughed. I thought of my father turning my tears to laughter and it was as if air had been blown into my chest and I felt as if I was going to explode. I never wanted to be like him. I wanted to be the opposite to him, do the opposite. Instead of tears to laughter, I wanted to turn laughter to tears, so I clenched up my fist and I punched him, and as my fist landed, it was my father's face. I could see it distorting under my fist and as the blood flowed from under my fist, and even more so when I pulled back, I thought, Job done.'

His forehead tips forward and rests against hers. A silent tear drips from the end of her nose, catching the sunlight as it falls.

'The boy staggered backwards and I walked away, away from him and away from me. I had no place to go, so I went to our accommodation. But as I walked, I was not on the ground; it was as if I was floating. My father opened the door to our unit before I even got there, and for once he was smiling, he looked so happy. He patted my shoulder. He took two beers from the fridge and he gave me one. The window was open, as usual, and I realised he had witnessed the whole thing and he was proud. It was one of the few times I can remember him opening up to me, giving me an honest response. All his stiff upper lip, all that British army reserve, gone, and for a bit, he was just my dad.' He shakes his head, still forehead to forehead with Irini. The movement is slow and he makes a noise as if sucking his teeth.

Irini does not feel the need to speak. His words soak into her. She feels his pain. She understands. She has lived that unloved life herself.

'Later, the boy's father came around along with the boy and they confronted my father with my behaviour. I stayed in my room; I was scared. Whilst the two fathers were talking, and then shouting, the boy excused himself to use the toilet but instead of going into the bathroom, he came down the corridor. He saw me looking out, as I had opened my bedroom door a bit to hear. He marched up to the door and pushed it open. I was trembling, but he had no fear of me. I had just caught him off guard and to prove it, he rabbit punched me in the nose and stomped away. He and his father left almost immediately. My nose was bleeding but I stuffed it with paper and willed it to stop. All I could think was that if my father saw my bleeding nose, he would stop being so proud.'

Irini nods her head. The foreheads come apart and they look up at each other, so very close. His eyes brim with tears; his age and hardness have all peeled away. Green eyes, straight nose, broad brow, and lines by his mouth twitching into dimples even in his sadness. The touch of his lips on hers is a healing balm, all the horrors falling away, washing her clean, back to being children, unspoilt, pure. It is the lightest kiss, like a butterfly landing, splaying its wings and taking to the air again. Then his cheek and ear brush her cheek and he nuzzles into the dip between neck and shoulder like a child.

It's difficult to tell if he is crying or not, but his body judders slightly now and again. Irini's face is wet with tears, for the hurt to this boy, for the hurt to her, for all they have endured at the hands of those who were meant to love and protect them.

Irini watches the movement of the sea, the expanse of blues and greens. Thoughts of Petta flit through her mind but what she is doing now, for herself, is more important. Breaking away these unspoken walls is not just for her but for them, their marriage, her son, their closeness. Something in the kiss was a sign, a confirmation that she is safe now and still loveable. It holds no guilt for her; it came from the purest of motives.

The streaks of bright, reflected sun appearing and breaking up on the crest of wavelets are being replaced by slices of dark water, undulating, shifting, changing. Far away, nearer the coast, a seagull soars high in the sky, and higher again, beyond where birds can fly is the trail of a plane long gone.

His voice is muffled as he speaks into her neck.

'After that, I knew how to be sure of his love, and the result is I am not a good man.' He pulls away to look in her eyes.

It would be easy to say she knows he is a mercenary but that would reveal her radio contact with the port police, so she says nothing.

'I tried very hard and I became an excellent bully. I did to the younger boys at boarding school twice what had been done to me. I did things that would scar them for life. I left one boy with a stutter, and the more people I hurt, the more the school wrote to or rang my father about my behaviour, and the prouder he seemed to be until the day I was eighteen and the door was opened and I was asked to leave, first by the school and then by my father.'

'Where did you go?' Irini asks, her voice small. Maybe he came to Athens. Maybe he was one of the people she knew on the street. Stranger things have happened.

'That was the question. Where could I go? If I had ever put my needs before his, he had called me selfish, so I had no idea what my needs were or even what I liked or wanted. To gain love, I had learned to be selfless in my portrayal of the son he wanted, the son that pleased him, but it was not who I was. I have no idea who I am. I was trapped in the person I had created to gain his love. It was the only thing I could do well. So I went where I knew I could be selfless, where every decision would be made for me and the person I had created would have a use. I replaced my father with the army.'

Irini nods. Their hands are still intertwined and they grow sweaty in the sun but neither of them let go; it is their safety line.

'My life with him, my father, was like living in a room where all the walls kept changing shape and the only window onto the outside world had distorted glass. Even though this was my reality, nothing seemed real. When I was at school, the whole military structure kept the pressure on, but he continued to add his distortions through letters and phone calls. So when I joined the army and both letters and phone calls suddenly stopped, and the walls became straight and the window clear, it was a shock and a liberty. I had found my perfect world, you understand?' He stops. His eyebrows have raised in the middle.

'That is how the streets felt for me. It was harsh and unforgiving and cruel, but at least it was constant and the rules were unchanging. I was not at the mercy of one other person and there was no pretence of love,' Irini agrees, frowning as she remembers.

'And I was good at it. I was good at taking orders, I took pride in being good at doing things others shied away from. I excelled. So when we were sent to do war games and the boys around me were shocked by the carnage, I just carried on in my own bubble, untouched by anything. It was man against man, army against army. I was promoted.'

'I can see how that could happen,' Irini says.

'It was real but it was not real. And I made a friend, the first and probably last, in my life. We did not speak much but somehow we knew each other. We were sent into a war zone together.' He begins to tell of their first deployment, a time when it was not man against man, a time when it was them against whoever – or whatever – they came across, and on that very first occasion, it was a small group of civilian houses.

In Irini's mind, it could be Greece that he is describing, with the barren soil, the dust, the heat, but he is careful not to say where it was. The pictures he draws are very real.

They were dropped outside a cluster of houses, crudely made, wooden-framed. The sound of shells was not so far away. Their job was to clear the area and return as quickly as possible to their platoon. They were advised that if there was anybody in the houses, they would probably give the appearance of being just farmers and their families, but they must clear the houses anyway. Who knows who is who in war? Children can carry bombs and women can hold guns, so clear them all. The shelling became more distant as they reached the edge of the cluster of houses. They were a group of four, so they split into twos, Sam with his friend, and they circled the outside of the houses. The dwellings were two storeys and appeared empty, windows broken, doors swinging open, chickens pecking outside the porches.

Sam heard the shouts of 'Clear!' as the other pair emerged from the first building. Gun in hand, he ran into the dwelling nearest to him, through the rooms downstairs, up the stairs, and down and out again. 'Clear,' he called. His friend had taken the next house so Sam skipped that one and moved to the one after it. The chickens continued to peck, a skinny dog stood still in the middle of the hamlet, and other than that, nothing stirred. Sam ran in through the broken door, a sweep of the downstairs rooms, furniture still there, even plates on the table as if a family had been about to eat, now sat all but empty, only serving dust. Up the stairs, a toy on the landing, plastic with wheels and a string to pull it by, a room with a blue-striped mattress on a bed and a pile of rags.

He was about to leave when he heard a whimper. Turning, something moved! He raised his gun. Held steady. Nothing to see. He waited for another movement. Camouflaged amongst the pile of rags and bedding, something stirred. He tensed, finger ready. It was a child, no more than three, maybe four, a girl in tattered clothes, big brown eyes. Such big, brown, soulful eyes. His training kicked in and the girl was cleared. She could have been rigged; you mustn't take the risk. Back down the stairs, he shouted out 'Clear!' to his comrade, and he ran, his friend in front of him, the other two in front again, all running down the street out into open countryside.

The force that hit him lifted him from the ground and pushed him back. He could not tell how far; several of his body lengths. The dust obscured all vision. It was a white-out. Crouching, he put his hand over his mouth, muffling his coughing. Sound was a target, too. With his jacket pulled over his nose, he waited for the debris to settle. From nearby came coughing and groans. A crater cut away the ground where the two soldiers ahead of him had been. Nearby was his friend lying on his back, also blown back by the blast. He was so relieved to see him alive, but the place wasn't safe and they must move quickly.

All senses alert, he crawled across to his friend.

'Come on; we are exposed.' He pulled at lapel of his friend's jacket and looked into his eyes and he noticed for the first time that they were brown. Brown like the girl's.

There had only been a second of eye contact with the little girl and it was only now that he recognised what he had seen. It was a look of relief, relief that someone had come to rescue her. As he looked into his friend's eyes now, there was also relief, but a different relief, and it was then that Sam saw that one of his friend's legs was gone and the foot missing from the other. The arm of his jacket lay some way away with his hand still in it. His friend smiled.

Clutching at him, Sam told him he was fine and his buddy smiled all the more. His last words were, 'Job done,' as if his own death was his aim.

It was as if someone had reached down inside of him and ripped out anything that was left of his heart. His friend lay motionless now. There was nothing he could do for him. It was then that it occurred to him that he had not checked that the girl was dead. One of the first things they were taught was to always be sure. Running back to the house he had cleared, he felt the shoulder of his jacket grow wet and realised he had been injured but he ran on, into the house and up the stairs. In one movement, he scooped up the little girl and ran with her in his arms, ran and ran, back to the rendezvous with the platoon and as he arrived, he fell onto his knees in front of the field doctor and begged and begged him to do something to help her.

The doctor and sergeant and all the uniformed man froze in their occupations and they looked at him with unbelieving eyes and open mouths and only then did Sam see the girl clearly. Perfect arms and legs, smooth and tanned, one white patent leather shoe still on with a sock that needed pulling up. Her flower-patterned dress, stained but pretty, her arms hanging loosely, and her neck unblemished. The rug of matted hair that hung over his arm was long and impregnated with dust and what was left of her head.

He had done that.

Sam's tears are silent.

They both stay quiet.

Until there is breath enough for words.

'I am not a good man,' he says, but Irini has no answer for him. He is talking about a child the age of her Angelos. She can feel all he is feeling, understand every twisted emotion he has grown up with, his hatred for his father, the distorted view he was left with. Every step of the way, she was in his shoes. But a child? Angelos. She sits back.

'I was a machine, Rini. Every step of my life, I was refining that machine - a machine that did not think but did as it was ordered, both in deed and emotion. But despite my training by my father, school, and army, my heart still raged against it.' Rini remains unmoved. 'I was discharged on medical grounds.' He is chewing at the side of his thumb and looking at the floor.

Medical grounds. Is that his excuse, his redemption? How insane does a person have to be to kill a child, and is it ever enough?

But then, how sane was she when she was homeless and how close did she come to killing people, other children? She clubbed someone on the back of the head who pushed her out of the way of some food she found. What if she had clubbed him too hard, what if he had fallen against something sharp? There were plenty of sharp things amongst the rubbish they were wading about in. And then there was the youth she stabbed. The youth who didn't actually do anything. It is not something she wants to talk about with Sam. After his tale, it is nothing, but the images and memories come of their own accord.

The sleep she woke from was deeper than normal. The corner she found herself in was warm by night and discretely hidden behind some shops. She was drawn from the depths of this slumber to find a stranger standing over her, one leg on either side. Alert before her eyes were fully open, she squirmed backwards from under his stance and onto her feet, ready to fight or run.

That was when she saw the second youth behind the first. He was chuckling to himself in the half-light of dawn, his features in high contrast from the cigarette lighter he had cupped in his hands as he lit up.

Irini looked from one to the other. None of their movements were hurried, nor manic, so they were probably not drug addicts. Their shirts were not silk, they did not wear cheap but ornate watches, and they were not out of their teens, so perhaps they were not pimps, either.

The alley that led out from the loading area behind the shops had only one way in and out. Industrial bins lined the walls and stacks of cardboard boxes, folded flat, awaited collection. It was a quiet, reclusive place to sleep, but now she was trapped. The youth nearest her took a step towards her, grinning as if in a game. His friend behind chuckled, equally amused. Skirting around him, her back up against the shop's back doors and walls, her feet stood on rotting vegetable leaves, packing tape, and broken glass. The skin was so thick on the soles of her feet that the glass did not penetrate except in the crease under the big toe on one foot and in the arch of the other. With her next step, glass dug in the crease under her little toes.

The pain tore through her, screaming for her to stop, pull out the slivers, take care of the wounds. But the youth was relentless, his steps steady towards her. With her back against the doors, she walked on her heels. The second man blocked her escape, a casual movement barring her exit, no intimidation attached. It was almost as if he just wanted the game to continue.

Then, with a sudden dash, she lunged past him. The first youth took a leap towards her, his friend stepped backwards, quickly, out of his way, and Irini fell into a doorway.

The first youth loomed over her, his face black against the dawn sky. A bird began to sing, and it seemed so out of place. With her hands behind her on the ground, she scuttled away from him out of the doorway, the back of her head sliding against the aluminium of an industrial bin. A cockroach crawled over her hand, broken glass dug in her palms, and then something metal, long, the right size to fit into her palm, came into her grasp. Her fingers curled around it. The youth leaned forwards over her, his thin, feathery attempt at a moustache curled over his top lip, making up in length what it lacked in density. His breath came quickly, his eyes shining. His friend stopped chuckling. This was the moment - was it a game or was it for real? His smile faded, his eyes grew dark, his decision apparent.

There was no thought involved; her legs worked without her say-so. She leaped to her feet and lunged at him, her metal weapon in her hand. She drove it forwards, into the softness of his stomach. He bent over her arm, his breath expelling. His friend dropped his cigarette, open-mouthed and stunned momentarily into rigidity until he rocked first forwards and then back, not sure whether to intervene or stay safe. Irini ran. Ran and ran. It was only when she stopped several streets away in the bushes of a small park that she looked down at her weapon, expecting to see blood, signs of the horror she had just committed.

It was a strange entanglement of relief, disbelief, and fear to see that there was no blood. She had stabbed him with a spoon, the head of which was now bent over.

Half an hour later, she saw the pair again, from a safe distance. This time, they were getting on a trolley-bus to the other side of Athens. Neither looked the worse for the encounter.

Thank goodness it had been a spoon! If it had been a knife under that bin, a knife in her hand instead, she too could have been a killer. As it was, he doubled over in pain and the result shocked her even though she did not puncture his skin. But she knows from experience that if you hit on someone's biggest fear, and you hit it hard enough, people will do anything.

Was what she did so far away from what he had done? It would be easy to say that her actions were in the moment, defensive moves to keep herself alive. But surely entering an enemy building with his head primed to obey or die and drilled with propaganda about bomb-rigged children must have put him into a place where everything he saw was a legitimate target and the threat of death.

Did he even have a choice? Wasn't the luxury of making decisions taken away from him the moment he was born to such a father?

She does not have that excuse. She was once loved and the children she fought with were not actually a direct risk to her life.

The clouds over the land behind him have grown and darkened in colour. A storm might take some of the heavy heat from the air but, please, not whilst they are at sea. Irini makes a little prayer to a God she long ago lost her belief in. Observing the shifts in the clouds and focusing on something other than death and blame is such a relief, she continues to stare beyond Sam's shoulders until finally he turns to look at what she is seeing.

'There is a storm coming,' he states.

Chapter 11

'Why don't you just go alongside and arrest him?' Petta's voice is not calm and he mops his brow with a handkerchief embroidered with two black butterflies.

Captain Yorgos wants to leave, but Marina keeps asking him questions. Is his boat seaworthy? How far will they have got in the time they have been gone? With each answer, he grows with importance until he is sitting upright and pulling his t-shirt to cover his stomach and picking the dirt from under his nails to make him look more respectable. Marina is fanning herself with a newspaper.

'People in Athens have taken an interest, and the decisions are not in our hands. We have to be patient,' Captain Demosthenes replies. He is calm, but he too is sweating in the heat. Picking up the remote, he presses the button to turn up the air conditioning but no matter how hard he presses, it is as high as it will go. He throws the remote back on his desk with disdain.

'This is not about who makes the decisions. This is about my wife.' Petta is a bigger man than

Demosthenes. He could use his height to intimidate the port police captain, but he doesn't. His t-shirt is slowly darkening with sweat between his pectoral muscles.

'I understand, Petta, but we have to follow orders.' Demosthenes' voice sounds sincere.

'What would you do if you were giving the orders?' Petta ruffles the hair of his child, who clings to his leg.

'I would probably put a vessel either side of the yacht and demand his surrender. With such a tactic, he would be unwise to refuse.'

'And if he did?' Petta is doing his best not to shout.

'Well, there is the problem. If there was no one else on board, we would open fire, shoot stern to bow on the diagonal. So you see the problem.' Demosthenes accepts an offer of coffee by a petty officer. Petta refuses.

When the coffee arrives, the port police commander takes his down the stairs and outside. Petta watches him through the window, drinking and looking out to sea and holding his elbows up so any breeze there is cools him.

'Drink something, Petta my love. You have eaten and drunk nothing all day,' Marina soothes, putting down the newspaper.

'Sometimes it is best not to take anything in when we are stressed,' Captain Yorgos offers her in an obsequious tone of voice.

Petta gives him a sideways grimace, but Marina thanks him for his kindness. Yorgos excuses himself to get the ashtray and when he comes back, he casually moves his chair a little closer to Marina.

'Marina, maybe we should take our minds off everything that is happening. I understand you have the corner shop in the village. Do you have land as well?' Yorgos asks.

Marina's look is blank.

'Petta, ask the port police what will make them take action,' she demands.

'Mama, I am afraid for them to take action now. They say they might have to use guns if he refuses to surrender.' A sparrow has landed on the palm tree outside the window, on a large feathery leaf that sways slightly with the contact. The bird does not sing, but Petta wonders if he would hear it even if it did, the cicadas are so loud. On the road that follows the harbour's edge, a moped putters by, a young man steering and a woman in black sitting sidesaddle behind him. She is wearing green slippers and her feet are crossed to hold them on as the soles flap with the speed.

'Well, surely the first thing to do is to ask him to surrender. Why don't they do that over the radio?' Marina says, ignoring Yorgos, who is trying to say something to her. Petta is quick to answer her.

'He says that he must obey orders from Athens. It is not up to him to make the orders now.' He watches Demosthenes walking up and down outside, and then he falls into a stare.

'*Panagia mou!*' Marina exclaims and stands up, bustles out the door of the corner office and over to the radio station and snatches the microphone from the operator's hand.

'Irini. Irini, are you there?'

'*Kyria*, you cannot do that.' The radio control man puts his hand out for the microphone.

Marina turns her back on him. 'Irini, Rini, can you hear me?'

'*Kyria*, I must insist.' The radio man stands and tries to take the microphone from her. Marina slaps his wrist.

'Rini, this is Marina. If you can hear me, ask that man who is with you if he will surrender.'

'*Kyria*, I really must insist.' The radio man takes hold of her wrist and tries to prise the microphone from her clenched hand.

'Mama, what are you doing?' Petta has hurried over to see what the fuss is about.

'I am making something happen.' Marina slaps at the radio operator's hands again. 'Ouch, you are hurting me. Don't you dare put your hands on me! Have you no respect?' The radio operator lets go of her wrist. 'How old are you? Seventeen, eighteen? You don't even look like you have started shaving yet. Well, I am old enough to be your mama, young man. By God, boy, if I had a wooden spoon on me now...' The radio man backs away, fear and disbelief all over his face, sweat running from his temples down his smooth cheeks. Perhaps he has a mother at home with a wooden spoon. Either way, it is clear she has touched a nerve.

'If you hurt my mama...' Petta stands in front of her and it is the radio operator who looks relieved.

'What on earth is going on?' Demosthenes puffs as he enters the office.

'Sir,' the radio hand begins to explain. But before any one can say any more, Captain Demosthenes assesses the situation and strides to the radio and turns it off.

'Right, explain,' he demands and everyone talks at once, but it is Marina's voice that comes across the clearest.

'These boys, they have no respect,' she barks. 'When I was their age, I already had one son and another in the grave. You children don't even know you are alive yet,' she says, turning on the young port policemen who have grouped together in solidarity.

'Please, please, this is an official office,' Demosthenes pleads. 'Come Marina, Petta. Let us take this outside so I can hear you without interruption.' He ushers them to the door and looks back into the room with a scowl, jabbing his finger at the radio operator and then at the radio. The young man jumps across to his station and turns the radio back on.

Captain Yorgos looks about the room, which seems empty now with Marina gone. Maybe he should go now. Maybe he could go to one of the kiosks, ring up the insurance company, explain the situation, and get the ball rolling. He supposes he

128

should really have let the Swiss people know that they were not sailing today, but what is the point of walking all the way down to the harbour just to let some people know that they will not be paying him anything today? So depressing. Although if he does go down to meet them, maybe he can persuade them to go sailing on another day if he gets his boat back. He lights up another cigarette.

Maybe this Marina could be a good bet. So there is a son and a daughter-in-law and even this little grandchild. He looks over to Angelos, who has slumped over Marina's large bag, fast asleep. But even with her family, she could be a good port in which to shelter from the storm of his old age. Irini already knows her place. Petta might prove a problem, but he seems like a passive, easy-going man, and the child, like all children, can be moulded or silenced.

Yes, Marina might be a very good port. He could still do his day trips but only at weekends, and also there would be the payoff of no longer having to pay Irini to clean his boats; after all, family is family. She could hardly charge him.

He settles back into his chair, flicking his ash onto the floor. Not a bad looking woman too: solid, good hips. It has been a while since he has thought of any woman in those terms; it's quite nice. He shifts about in his chair, but he can tell nothing has stirred. He breaks wind instead.

Chapter 12

The next hour on the boat feels like an eternity. The coastline seems to pass more slowly although they have not diminished their speed. The port police have gained on them but almost imperceptibly. The sun's steady, incessant heat is relentless and the only movement for a while is a hand across a forehead or a thumb across a drip on the end of a chin. Irini has considered jumping again, but if he can shoot a child, perhaps he would not hesitate to shoot her. It seems so far removed from that kiss they shared, that moment of safety and acceptance. She wants to return to that, that sense of *everything is going to be alright*.

She wonders why the port police don't do anything but at the same time, she has a sense of relief that they haven't. She is not ready yet. Would it be worth the risk to call them again to get someone to telephone Stathoula? There is no way that it will cross Petta's mind. She glances at her watch. He will probably have been down to the port by now, looking for her. Seeing the boat missing he will have found Yorgos, and know everything. Poor Petta. Thank goodness Angelos is too young to understand.

She walks up to the bow, leans against the pulpit, and watches the water being split by the stem. Sam remains in the cockpit, his head hanging, his forearms on his knees. He was, and is, asking her for forgiveness, but why? The tension between them now has reignited her fear. With the pressure on her to forgive, to release him from the painful place he is in, isn't he putting her in the same position his baba put him in? She could say the words, but she knows she would not have feeling behind them. Lying would be the best move, but those days of ingratiating herself to her yiayia, to anyone, to stay alive, she is not sure she is prepared to return to that.

To hell with him! Let him suffer. If he had given half the thought she is giving him to the little girl, that child would be alive now and maybe he wouldn't be in this situation.

Unless, of course, things had been different and the child really had been strapped up with explosives.

A shiver starts in her shoulders and runs down her spine.

It would be nice if a dolphin would come now, release her mind of all this. Leaning over, she looks deeper into the surf, the spray catching her face, refreshing and cool. He is no different than Pavlov's dogs, salivating at the sound of a bell. The spray wets her t-shirt and she stands straight. The wind and the sun dry it in minutes. If he is only a

Pavlov's dog, what really does she not forgive? What is the stumbling block?

Holding onto the pulpit rail, she leans backwards, the sun on her face and her eyes closed. The stumbling block is forgiving him for allowing himself to be made into one of Pavlov's dogs, for telling her that it is possible. She does not want to know that a man can be conditioned to react in such extreme ways even when that reaction is against his nature.

She does not forgive him for showing her that the last shred of what she would call humanity can be stripped from a person and they can commit such atrocities even when their nature tells them otherwise. That is what she cannot forgive. For what is true of one will be true of another. What if she ever has to wear his shoes, or those like them? She does not want to know what she could be capable of. The emotional scars she has already cut deep enough and are enough to live with.

Damn him.

Damn him.

No, love him.

It is the only way to undo such evil.

She grips her left breast to feel her heart beating beneath. It aches for people like Sam, and it aches for all of mankind. It aches for the horror of life, the ugliness the world makes possible and for the fact that people make that horror manifest.

Then she lets go of her own skin and looks down into the water. She hates him.

Arms across her chest, she takes her time to wander back and lies down on her back under the boom, looking up at the mast. She does not want to be near him. With a glance, she sees he is standing, leaning against one of the stays at the back of the boat, his hips pushed forward, one hand to his groin, his back to her.

If she were a man, she would probably not use the inside toilet either but in this moment, this base action describes all he is.

Her eyes close and she drifts. When she wakes, he is lying next to her, not looking up the mast, but at her. If anyone else were there to take a picture of them in the moment, with the sun shining, the sea a calm endless blue, two people lying prone, only their heads turned as they look at each other, the result might be an advert for sailing, or for Greece, full of fun, friendly people and long, warm nights.

She turns her head away from him, closes her eyes again, tries to shut out the chaos of emotions he creates.

'Tell me about your village or how you met your husband? Something normal,' he says.

'Normal. You want normal? After stealing this boat because you are running from something, taking me as a hostage at gunpoint, belittling the value of my life down to a shrug, you now want normal?' She has run out of energy to be with him. She will lie here for a moment or two, longer if necessary. He will, in all probability, drift into sleep in the afternoon sun and when he does, she will

133

soundlessly slip into the water and before he wakes, she will be far away.

Maybe a story will send him to sleep.

'Okay. How I met Petta,' she introduces her story.

'With the hell I had lived on the streets, I was broken. I didn't believe in society, or people, or care, love, friendship, nothing. I felt stripped of, how do I say, stripped of any connection, a place in the world. All around me, I saw the evidence of how thin the coating of civilisation was. I saw the characters people could become if they too ended up clinging onto the edges of life as I had done. It made them appear like they had two faces, the real one hidden, the polite one doing the bidding.'

As the day has progressed into the afternoon and the temperature has risen, the deep of the blue sky has intensified; it is almost purple.

'I was amazed that my cousin cared enough to take me in. I did not trust her, nor her sister. I wondered what their motives were, but they had known my parents and, more importantly, my yiayia was also their yiayia, although they saw less of her than I did, living with her every day.'

Irini turns her head to see if he is asleep yet and flinches to find him staring at her. She turns away and continues looking at the sky.

'I fought their care. I tested it and threw tempers. But they, both Stathoula and Glykeria, stayed calm and constant and I began to slot back into the workings of a household. You know:

washing up, doing the laundry, taking showers, all of which were big things to me. On the streets, I had done none of those things for three years. Once back in company, I thought that their expectations that I should be doing these things were a pressure, like the pressure Yiayia put on me to not be me. It felt like being asked to give up who I was.

'One day, I just did it automatically. I picked up my clothes from the floor and took them and put them in the washing machine along with Stathoula's clothes from the basket.' Her voice softens, quiets. The words come out more slowly.

'It didn't even occur to me what I had done until I went into the kitchen and Stathoula smiled at me in this particular way she has, as if to say 'well done,' and 'I love you,' all at once.'

She puts her hands above her head, relaxed, the light wind blowing across her armpits, cooling and silky.

'I don't really remember a lot of details after that until the day Stathoula got me a job. I was terrified. To go out into the world. They would see me for the fake I was, the street dweller, the problem. The first job was just handing out leaflets for a fast food place. Stathoula went with me and did not leave me until she was sure I was comfortable. The place I stood to give them out was down in Monastiraki, do you know it? Next to Plaka, near the Acropolis.' She turns to look at him.

'No,' he replies.

'Well, it doesn't matter. It is just a busy shopping place. Stathoula went shopping, so every couple of hours, I would see her walking past. But no one shops for eight hours, so I knew she was really there for me. At the time, I wondered why Stathoula kept walking past. Did she not trust me? Did she think I was going to run away? That evening, Glykeria served a meal and afterwards brought out a cake she had made and iced, with the word Irini on it. The icing had all run, and when I read it, I thought it said Irida. Do you know Irida? She was a goddess in ancient Greece. Well, not exactly a goddess, but I don't know the right word. Anyway, she was my favourite and she makes the rainbows. In Greek, the coloured part of the eye is called irida, from her. She still calls me that, Glykeria. Always Irida, not Rini or Irini.'

For a moment, she says nothing, remembering Glykeria calling her Irida. Stathoula called her it too but soon went back to Rini. It became something personal between her and Glykeria and it gave a sense of place, a sense of belonging.

'Go on,' he encourages. He is showing no signs of being sleepy yet.

'I had a series of short-term jobs, one for a week, another for a weekend. I think Stathoula thought it was the easiest way to ease me back into the world. Then one day, on a break from one of these jobs, I went for a walk in Plaka.'

Chapter 13

The square at Monastiraki was a cauldron of nationalities, a morass of merchandise, a nucleus of impromptu happenings. Entry to the square was impossible without pushing past one of many fruit barrows that blocked the roads that bled outwards from the paved hubbub. These hand carts on metal wheels, piled high with pyramids of fruit, all but formed a barricade that blocked day trippers exiting from the metro or ambushed the shoppers coming down from Athens' central square of Syntagma. Some of the flat backs supported elaborate water fountains that cascaded into metal moats designed to keep fresh the coconut meat being chipped from their hairy shells with large knives. The stall holders called their wares in loud baritone voices, vying with one another to be first in line to skim the fat wallets brought by ever-eager pedestrians.

It was the feel of the square that Irini liked. When she was homeless, her nimble fingers also liked the easy pickings of the fruit stalls. Not the bananas, which were in bunches, nor the grapes, no matter how sweet, but the pears and the apples. One grab and you were away. One from each barrow, tucked under her shirt or down into the pocket she had improvised inside the front of her skirt. Once round the square and she had enough to feed her for a couple of days if nothing else turned up.

But those days were gone, thank goodness. Now she worked at a kafeneio, making coffee for old men. She had a home and family, a mattress to sleep on with clean sheets, running water, electricity, and clean walls. Now there was no need to be sly as she passed the barrows; she had no need to be afraid. In her pocket, a *tiropita*, not even a bought *tiropita* but one Glykeria made last night, the feta crumbled into the filo pastry with a sprinkle of herbs. The smell when it was baking had drifted throughout the house and was equally as tempting as the *stifado* dinner that was cooking alongside it, the aromas mixing as they leaked into the warm night air.

Taking out her pie, she watched the backpackers file out of the metro, looking left and right around the barrows, trying to place themselves in the kaleidoscope of the square. The streets that led up to central Athens were lined with expensive clothes shops, the occasional oriental rug shop pressed in between, and the odd quality fur shop that looked out of place in the scorching summer heat. One or two art shops offering sculptures of broken Ionic columns and paintings of Olympian disc throwers also staked a claim and left their doors open with well-dressed experts loitering in them to explain their finer pieces to potential customers who dared to glance in the windows.

Another wide street led away from the square to climb a slope. The left side of this street boasted archaeological ruins, fenced off and mostly ignored, as this was the base of the Acropolis and higher up, grander things awaited. Where this road joined the square, street sellers displayed their goods on unlicensed tables. The illegal aspect, the insecurity, the risk taking, was what gave the place a feel of youthfulness, possibilities, creativity, life!

An African man selling fake designer handbags stood next to a young mother with jewellery fashioned from ring pulls saved from drink cans. Her nose was pierced and she had a tattoo on her thumb. Her child stayed close. Next to her, an old Greek man sold things that looked like he found them in his attic. He offered, in an ornate gold plastic frame, a print on canvas of a grand old English king. Next to that was a red plastic telephone box, the height of a whiskey bottle, with the words *Jack Daniels* where the word *Telephone* should have been. There was a futuristic orange telephone, all curves, from the 1960s, a baseball glove with 'I love Greece' woven on the back, and a chess set with three pawns missing. He sold things that Irini had no idea she wanted until she saw them. She picked up an enamelled ladybird keyring which was particularly pretty and a paper knife with a totem pole handle that might be useful.

Next was a man who challenged passers-by to a game of *tavli* for a small wager. He was in the middle of a game, concentrating, a small crowd gathered around him and his young opponent.

These street sellers were almost her friends when she was homeless, at least in as far as they weren't her enemies. But unlike her, they had places to stay and ways to make money, even if they were illegal. She could only steal and, at the time, she looked up to them as leading lives to which she could aspire.

As she took out her *tiropita*, which Glykeria had wrapped in a linen napkin, it occurred to her that in the hierarchy of life, the unspoken pecking order, she was now one above these people. It stopped her from taking her first bite as she looked around. Now she could see the bitten nails, the unwashed hair, the cheap plastic shoes, where before she saw the t-shirts without holes, the fact that they had shoes at all, and the wasted money that had manifested itself as tattoos, and lipstick on the women's mouths.

But still, the feeling was there, the tension of suppressed youthful energy that society contains and, in this area, found an outlet through the street vendors' creativity.

A crowd was gathering in the square's centre. Through the crowd, she could see a group of boys with a cassette player, the volume of which was turned up as they began to dance. The spectators formed a circle around the boys, growing thick, and cheers and waves of excitement ran through the crowd.

Irini spotted a child, his way of moving and dress familiar. His feet were swift and silent as he made his own shoeless dance, weaving through the crowd. He had hands like moth wings, too gentle to feel and with no flamboyancy to attract anyone's attention. But like a moth drawn to the light, his hands were pulled, always, towards the open handbags and bagging jacket pockets. He created his own rhythm but he made sure no one noticed his performance and as the cassette player's melody wound to its conclusion, the boy, like a puff of air on gossamer, was gone. Flitting, no doubt, to another blossom, to deflower another innocent tourist.

The *tiropita* was delicious. Maybe Glykeria would teach her how to make them; then it could be something for her to contribute to the household.

In total, there are eight streets that exit the square and it is what Irini considered to be the eighth street that she always used to gravitate to before her yiayia's funeral and, again, she felt drawn there now. It led to the area called Plaka.

Irini turns to see if Sam is asleep, but he hasn't taken his eyes off her.

'You know Plaka?' she asks. 'The Neighbourhood of the Gods,' she says, looking into his eyes. He doesn't respond. 'Oh come on, you must know it. Everyone who has been to Athens knows it. It is all very old, near the Acropolis. Narrow streets.

Even now, if you know where to go up near the top, there are tiny whitewashed huts and old people trying to live like it is the olden times with a goat tethered to a stake and a dozen chickens. No?'

Sam rolls his head against the teak decking to say *no* but his eyes are alive, the green reflecting the energy she is portraying. The corners of her mouth turn down and her eyebrows raise at her disbelief that he has not been there, and she continues her story.

This eighth street was crammed with narrow shops. No space had been left unexploited by the individual traders. Cellars had been converted, corridors turned into narrow emporiums, alleyways roofed and painted, shop fronts divided into two to squeeze in one more trader. Sometimes you stepped up to a shop, or descended into a cellar. Some were along corridors, the shop itself hidden around the back of other buildings, and each sold their own variation of fashion: studded leather jackets, tartan miniskirts, corseted dresses with layers of netting under the micro skirts which were displayed on shop dummies with broken fingers, paint-peeling faces and matted wigs. Others displayed t-shirts with slogans, broomsticks shoved through their arms and then suspended on string from nails hammered into whatever is solid. Thigh boots were displayed on amputated mannequin legs topped with officer's hats liberated from armies all around the world. It sparked her imagination and thrilled her senses as incense perfumed the air and music drifted from each shop.

Irini had a sense of belonging here. Here, the rejected was given new life, the mismatched found a home. In these streets, it was possible for the alternative: to avoid becoming mainstream.

At the entrance to this road, instead of a fruit barrow, stood a man with a stall on spindle legs. With a quick movement, he could close his stall like a book, the legs falling alongside and, slinging the strap that was stapled to the wooden construction over his shoulder, he could be closed for business and running in less than three seconds. She knew; she had seen him do it when the police used to raid for the unlicensed, trying to clear the street traders on a regular basis to clean up the area.

He was still there, the man with the folding shop, selling oversized cigarette papers and silver jewellery that turned your fingers black. Bald at the front, his receding hair was held in a ponytail down his back. He had a darkness around his deep-set eyes that did not look healthy and his shaved chin was smooth and slightly shiny. She had never spoken to him, but she had heard him speak.

Behind where he always stood was a recess in the wall. It was the perfect fit when a police raid came and she needed to get out of the way. It was also a good place to eat her stolen fruit and still be able to watch the world whilst remaining hidden. She stepped next to it. It smelt of urine and looked a lot dirtier than she remembered.

The man with the folding shop served someone. He was short-tempered and could not be bothered with the customer's questions. His accent when speaking Greek was thick.

He was English.

It struck her as odd that someone with such a privileged background, brought up in England that has a welfare system, should end up selling cigarette papers off an illegal stand on a dingy street in Athens. She could remember thinking when she first heard him speak, in her fruit-stealing days, that, surely, when you have such a privileged upbringing, you must only end so low by choice.

At this point in her story, Irini stammers and a rush of heat climbs her neck. She looks over to Sam, the English pirate, but there is no sign that he has taken this comment personally and so she continues.

The first shop, down this street that she loved, sold shoes. Ridiculous shoes with platform soles and high heels, boots that did up with buckles up to the knees and heels so high that twisting an ankle would be an ever-present danger. She liked that the designers had stepped out of the conventional and looked at footwear with a disregard for tradition.

The next shop was in a basement. It sold French horns and bagpipes, vinyl records and medals. It never appealed much. Beyond that was a girl who designed her own clothes. Very friendly but never seemed to sell much.

144

And so it went on. And on. Until the street abruptly ended where another street crossed it. The land opposite was bare earth offering the occasional top of an ancient wall, waiting for an archaeologist to come and investigate. The house on the right corner was private and the place on the left, a taverna.

Her *tiropita* was all gone and her break must surely have been over.

Loud voices at the taverna made her casually glance over. One of the men speaking was taking a bouzouki out from a hard case. She loved music; she would stay just for the first chord. The spindly tree she leant against gave her shade. The paving flags beneath it cracked and raised, roots forcing their way through, demanding room. She shifted her feet to find flat stones, greater comfort. From practice, she knew how to use the tree to half-obscure her, leaning against it, melting into its shape.

A chord was struck and an old *rebetika* song echoed across and back from the ancient ruins. Someone began to sing and then a tall man with broad shoulders and narrow hips with his back to her stood, moved by the music, his arms thrown out to the side. His dark hair was wavy and long enough to touch his collar. Crumpled jeans suggested he was in need of an iron, or an ironer, but his boots, with Cuban heels, had been carefully polished. He moved with joy and with a certain delicacy that well-built men sometimes have. It was as if he was full of helium and was having trouble staying grounded, bouncing on his toes from step to step, his neck loose, his head rolling in response to the rest of his body. The sun drenched him and the musician. It was as if he was rejoicing to be alive, like a butterfly caught in a draft, blowing happily, with rhythm, whichever way the wind blew.

Then he turned.

His eyes, creased in the corners, danced without seeing, lost to the rhythm. His chest expanded in his jubilation and his soft smile was that of a man without a care in the world, and the ground shifted beneath Irini's feet. He was the inverse of all the darkness she had seen and felt. He was on fire with being alive and she saw how different the world could be depending on how you chose to view it.

'I don't know how long I was standing there staring at him dancing. I didn't even hear one song become another and the rhythm change, but all of a sudden, I was snapped out of my wonderful thoughts as, in time to the music, he stepped towards me. His hand was held out, inviting me to join him. His arm slipped over my shoulders and side by side, we danced, our free arms outstretched and I become part of his joy. His exuberance was infectious, the world open to me, and anything was possible. And what was possible, became.'

Lost in the feelings her story evokes in her, she doesn't move, lying there enjoying all the wonders of Petta, all he has done for her just by breathing, just by being alive, just by loving her.

What was possible was love, and it was his love that healed so many of her wounds, all except the ones that were too much for him to bear to hear, or ones she thought were too harsh to tell. But even without knowing everything, he has pulled her from her melancholy into a way to live life without sadness and for that, not only does she love him but she is grateful. He saved her.

She turns to look at Sam.

Chapter 14

With her heart full of love for Petta, it is easy to feel sorry for Sam. There is something about him that is almost like looking into a mirror to a time before her dancing butterfly settled into her life. If Sam has a wife, a family, he is a long way from home and heading even further away from England to Casablanca. It must be tearing him apart, and it's not as if it is just distance, either; he is being hunted by the police and must feel so very, very alone.

He has not fallen asleep. Instead, he is very much awake and he is still looking at her.

'Why Casablanca?' Her question comes out softly.

'I am a mercenary.' He says it like it is the most normal thing in the world. Irini raises her eyebrow, not sure how shocked she should pretend to be to avoid suspicion. She lets her mouth fall open a fraction, too.

It seems she has judged it right, as he continues. 'I have contacts there. It is a good place to get my next job.' He speaks as if the words have nothing to do with him, and some of the spark that was lighting up his eyes grows dark. He slaps at something on his neck.

'It's a long way to Casablanca. We will hit Italian or Libyan water first and as far as I know, Greece is on good terms with both. The port police will alert them. Don't you think Turkey would be safer? Closer. Less friendly?' Irini offers.

'I'm trying to avoid too many borders. I have no passport; it was taken.' He rolls onto his back, his hand to the wound on his side. 'How long do you think it will be before we leave Greek waters?'

Irini blinks and then closes her eyes at the question and tries to conjure up a map but has no way of knowing any of the distances.

'I really have no idea. A day, no, more. Two perhaps. There are charts below.'

His hair is sleek against the teak deck and shimmers as he shakes his head slowly. In line of sight behind his head is the mast and then the pulpit at the front of the yacht. The chrome of these railings is reflecting the sun, throwing rays back at them that cut across his profile, blurring his lips and chin. Whatever was irritating his neck returns and he skims it away with his fingers.

'You want to go back to Casablanca to take another job?' Irini asks.

'You mean "why haven't I changed my plans now I have met you?"' Sam scoffs.

Irini does not like the way he turns from friendly to cruel so suddenly. Just as she begins to feel she knows him, he then stabs with his words. He must be very frightened to be so defensive and she cannot help the anger it ignites within her.

But maybe she did expect that to some degree. Their meeting has certainly changed her. The past has become a little more explainable, the events on the streets a little less personal. She certainly feels less removed from people, more normal.

'Well no, of course not. But maybe you have more to offer the world than you think,' she defends and he turns back onto his side to look at her.

'You think?' He smirks.

'Yes.' She leaves the one word to hang there, open and honest.

'I think that is very easy for you to say from the comfort of your life that is full of love and support.'

'Love and support will come if you are brave enough to stay still somewhere,' Irini says, aware that her voice is just slightly sulky.

He laughs. 'You think your village will open their arms to me, do you? Offer me their friendship and support?' He laughs again. Irini rolls from her side onto her back, lies still for a minute and then sits up, her arms around her bent knees.

'I think you are being unkind.' Her mouth pinches shut; her eyes are slits against the sunlight.

'I told you I was not a nice man, or did you think you had changed that, too?' He is playing now, but he is playing on his own at her expense. She is the toy.

150

'That is just plain nasty.'

He doesn't answer her.

'I think you are scared in case I am right. I think to stay anywhere to find out if you would get support and care is the ultimate fear for you, in case you get rejected all over again,' Irini says, keeping as much harshness out of her voice as she can, but her jaw tightens when she has finished speaking and she finds she is grasping her knees tighter than is necessary.

'Which is why I don't.' Sam sits up too, resting on his arms behind him.

'But you could.' Irini turns to look at him. 'You could try it once and see what the world thinks of you and if it doesn't work out, then you could return to Casablanca.'

He looks out to the horizon. She follows his gaze. Somewhere beyond the curve of the earth in that direction is Crete and then Libya.

'Do you know how many islands there are in Greece?' Irini asks, but does not wait for an answer. 'Six thousand, but only a couple of hundred have people on them, and less than a hundred have a lot of people on them.' She waits for this to sink in.

'You see what I am saying?' she asks.

'You are saying something?' he answers. He sounds amused.

Letting go of her legs, her knees fall to one side and she turns to face him. The sun's rays are still glinting off the chrome work at the bow and it creates a halo of light down one side of his face. A dark side and a light side.

'You can do it.' Her feet tap, her arms fidget, an excitement runs through her. 'You can start again, take any island you want, choose a new name, and have a whole new life.' She smiles. It feels like such a perfect solution. He says nothing. 'Tell me how you would like it to be if you had a whole new life to invent.' She can hardly sit still. This is his solution.

With his eyes focussed down on the deck, he draws his feet in towards him, his hands clasping around them.

'It would be easy,' she says. 'We could sail to an island of your choice...'

'And what about the port police? They are just going to watch me jump off the boat and do nothing about it?'

'No, you could wait till dark...'

'You think they would stop watching the boat in the dark? You think they would not be looking for someone jumping in and swimming?' Sam says.

Irini thinks. 'Here's what you could do. You could slip into the water as it grows dark and work your way down a line that we tow behind us and when you are ready to let go, just let go. The port police will be watching the boat and they will not notice you some distance away, swimming quietly to shore.' She smiles her triumph and holds her arms out, palms up at the simplicity of the solution.

He looks up from the decking and makes eye contact. That sad look is back, and something else that she can only describe to herself as a yearning. But a yearning for what, she cannot tell. A new life maybe?

'What do you think?'

He shrugs his shoulders.

'Oh, we are back there, are we, where a life is worth nothing more than a shrug?' With these words, she looks to the stern. The port police have advanced a little bit closer, but they still pose no immediate threat. How will it all end? Is he to be arrested and put in handcuffs? Why have they not come alongside and done that already?

'I'm glad you didn't,' Sam says unlocking his arms, his posture opening out, the scars on his chest all visible, the thin skin puckering across his stomach and the chords in his neck still tense.

She knows he is talking about her intention to jump. Is he glad because she is still with him on the boat or just glad that he didn't have to shoot her?

Chapter 15

'How long before you got married?' Sam remains seated but stretches upwards until his bandaged midriff pulls taut, reminding him that he needs to heal, and his body retracts, his hand going protectively to his side.

'Not long. We saw each other in Athens for a couple of weeks, and then he was offered a job on Orino Island, his home village. Well, it wasn't so much a job as the loan of a taxi-boat with permission to run it as a service. It had all its licences and things, so it just made sense. Petta did that for a year. I got a job at a bar but it didn't last. The taverna was closed for illegalities, but then it re-opened and I got my job back because someone gave the men with power a big fat bribe, but they closed it again later and by that time, it was summer and all the jobs on the island were taken, so I didn't work.'

'How does that answer my question?' Sam asks but he is smiling. This is his humour.

'Well, it was because we only had the one job between us that we couldn't afford to get married. But then, through an extraordinary turn of events,

Petta found his birth mama. He's adopted; she couldn't keep him. Anyway, he found her and she invited us to the village to live with her. So then. It was then that we got married, in the village. Everyone in the village helped us out. We had tables in the square. It was lovely.'

She turns away from him slightly. He does not fit with these thoughts. That is her life with Petta, and she is not sure that he is welcome there.

Something tickles her arm. Without looking, she rubs it away to find it is Sam's fingertips, almost hovering over her skin, so light.

'What?' she asks.

'I just wanted to touch you. You know, feel your warmth, the softness, know you are real,' Sam says. She cannot tell if it is a joke or not so she tuts and frowns in a light-hearted way. It would be better if it was a joke.

'If I was to sum up being a mercenary in two words,' he speaks as if it is a secret, 'I would say *Idiots* and *Cold, hard, metal*.' Irini is about to point out that is four words when he adds, 'And you are neither an idiot, nor are you cold and hard.'

She swallows. The hairs on her forearm stand on end. Her stomach flips and she twists her tongue on the roof of her mouth, trying to relieve the dryness. She is not sure whether to be afraid or flattered.

'The army provided no direct support, just a lot of leaflets and telephone numbers, charities, do-gooders.' His lips curl over the words. 'After asking the right people, I found that my father had been posted out in the East somewhere. I was discharged without an address to go to and I knew no one. No one at all.' He is still touching her. He doesn't speak quickly, but there is an urgency in his voice, as if this is something he needs to tell.

'I slept under a bridge the first night. Woke up thinking the trucks running overhead were tanks, looked everywhere for my rifle.' He sniggers, but there is something self-critical in the laugh. Irini frowns and runs her left hand under her short, dark hair at the back. It is wet at the nape of her neck where she has been sweating. Her right arm she does not move, allowing the tips of his fingers continued contact.

'Anyway.' He shifts his position. His finger slides across her skin and his hand wraps around her forearm, his thumb rubbing across the muscle and back. 'Long story short. Met a man in a pub and he made a joke about joining the foreign legion, so I did.' This time, his laugh holds only sadness and he dips his head toward her, watching his hand caressing her skin. There are more scars on the back of his neck that she had not noticed before, thin and faded.

'You know there are forty-eight thousand professional soldiers?' His words are almost a whisper.

'Is that what they call mercenaries now?' Irini does not feel at all comfortable with him bowed before her like this. She needs to either enclose him within her arms and rock him or he needs to sit up.

'We are the biggest force in some places, outnumbering the countries' forces. They rely on us.' With these words comes energy; he does sit up, his back straight, and he lets go of her arm, which tingles with the memory of his touch. 'It's an industry that's worth two billion a year.'

The hard veneer has slipped back over his features. She has lost him again.

'Green berets, ex S.A.S., SEALS, the elite. Average pay used to be two-hundred-and-fifty to one thousand quid a day. Tax free.'

Irini converts the sum into euros in her head and a little gasp escapes her. 'But then they realised that instead of the Australians and the Americans and the English, they could use the Chileans, the Filipinos, the Nepalese, and the Bosnians. Those guys will work for twenty quid a day, and they're happy with it. It kicked the guts out of the industry.' And, as if to demonstrate, his spine curves and his stomach collapses inward, the bandage around his side crumpling on itself.

His face also sags, the muscles lifeless, dimples gone, mouth formless.

'I work alongside English guys in their early forties, ex-army, having a mid-life crisis.' He sniffs and then snorts. 'That or they are kids who have joined the army at seventeen and done their four years' military experience so they can join a contract company. The podgy middle-agers are coming to war instead of buying a red sports car and the kids are just looking for the big payouts. Most of them joined the army so young, they don't really know what civilian life is. Either way, none of them should be there.'

'I always presumed mercenaries were convicts on the run. You know, bad guys that were hiding,' Irini says, but she is wondering if he is one of the 'kids' who doesn't know what civilian life is really like.

What she said seems to have amused Sam and he laughs until he has to hold his bandaged side. His dimples deep on either cheek take longer to fade than his smile.

'You have to be Interpol-checked these days. They turn down eight out of ten men. They look for non-commissioned officers with supervisory experience. There are no leaders, no one to tell you what to do. You have to think for yourself, make decisions. Anyone going in there with a lust for combat, which there are, occasionally, psycho lads thirsting to do harm, quickly get let go or end up dead.'

Irini nods but she can't understand why anyone would want to live in such a world.

'As mercenaries, we do not clear houses.' Sam looks her in the eye. He seems to be forcing the point that he has chosen not to be party with such action. His words are clipped. 'As part of a private security company, we conduct inherently military operations, but we do not conduct offensive operations. We do not hunt down terrorists. We detect, defer, and defend against threats for the client, whoever they may be, person or post.'

The hard veneer is not there. She has not lost him, but he has stepped into another world, a world of jargon and precise language. This man she could imagine not only shooting her but cutting her from stem to stern if the situation required it.

'If we get into gun fights, we are not doing our jobs properly and we need to re-think. We give operational support to legitimate governments.'

His manner sends a shiver down her and she looks away.

She can see no future for him. If he just goes from one job to the next, when will he have a normal life? What chance will he have of finding a wife and having children, and what happens when he gets old? Where will he call home? If indeed he makes it to old age.

'You don't think starting again is a better idea?' Irini looks to the stern. The port police are inching their way towards them. If they are closing the gap, presumably they have a plan, but if they have a plan, why do they not just carry it out? Sam looks too.

'Frogs, eh?' he says with a smirk.

'What do you mean?'

'How do we know when the water is too hot?'

'What?'

'Or the police too close?'

'Oh, I see.' She looks again. They are close enough now to make out some detail. 'What will happen when they get too close?'

'They'll try to arrest me.' Sam sounds quite calm.

'So why don't you slip away now, start a new life? Could you swim to shore?'

He judges the distance. His lips purse and he nods his head.

'Probably, but a new life to do what?'

'Have a family?' Irini suggests.

'Most of the men I work alongside have families.'

'Really?' It is beyond her imagination.

'Why not? The rotations are usually only three or six months. Short stints. It's not like the SEALs, for example. They do anything up to fifteen, and you would not be surprised at them having a family, a wife waiting, would you? So with mostly short deployment and, if you do get longer contracts, significantly better rest periods, it attracts a lot of married men.'

'Do they have children?'

'Of course. Why wouldn't they?' Sam seems to find her amusing.

'Do they tell their children what they do?'

'Some of them do, some of them don't.'

'It would be hard enough for a wife, but how would a child cope with the thought that every time their baba goes off to work, they might not come back?'

Sam shrugs.

'Not really my problem,' he says and goes to sit in the cockpit. Irini notices that he stays low as he moves. Does he expect the port police to have a sniper take a shot at him?

Chapter 16

'Everything alright?' Yorgos asks Marina. They are still at the kiosk in Saros, just along from the port police offices. Yorgos grips the tubular tin of chocolate wafer biscuits he has bought tightly, the rounded metal cool against his palm.

'Oh yes. I just needed to call Costas to go in and mind the shop. I remembered that we have a delivery coming, so it seemed like the only option.'

'Very wise. I also imagine your customers expect you to be open.'

'I imagine this news has travelled like wildfire, Captain Yorgos, and they will not expect the shop to be open at all.'

'Please, just Yorgos, no need to call me Captain.' He pops off the lid off the chocolate wafer sticks and offers her the tin with a broad smile.

She waves her hand over them as a refusal and looks down the street toward the port.

'No need to starve yourself. Keep your strength up.' He offers them again.

'No thank you, Captain. I don't like that particular biscuit.' Marina pays for the phone call and begins to walk away.

Yorgos looks at the open biscuits. Maybe he could get a refund. The man in the kiosk, who has been watching the exchange has one eyebrow raised. The captain decides against even asking and hobbles after Marina, trying to stuff the lid back on.

'I take it that it is a good-sized farm you've got?' He opens the conversation. It is only responsible to know what he is getting himself into.

'Oh you know, about average.' Marina sounds distracted.

'It is too much for just your son.' Making it a statement rather than a question is a good line, show her how another man around the place could be useful.

'What makes you say that? He manages just fine.' Marina is walking faster back to the port police office than she did going.

'Ah, I know that often, we men pretend we are fine when really we could do with a bit of help.' If he rolls onto the outside of his foot as he walks, for some reason the pain in his thigh is less.

'Do you need help, Captain Yorgos?' Marina stops walking. Yorgos' relief comes out as a puff through bulging cheeks.

'No, no.' He tries to laugh lightly but he also has a need to cough, and the cough wins.

'Good. Then I will leave you here.' And she marches off toward the port police, leaving Yorgos leaning on his knees, coughing and holding tightly to the biscuit tin.

Irini stays where she is under the boom. It's been a while since she has talked to the port police. Perhaps she should make contact. Go below, use the toilet, and make a call.

'Just going below,' she tells Sam as she stands. But he is not in the cockpit where she expected to see him. Even with both hands as a sun visor, the brightness that reflects from the boat's white gel-coat makes scanning the deck tricky. With a second sweep, it is clear that he is not there. She dips her head into the hatch, blinks a few times so her eyes can adjust to the relative darkness. The intense sunlight through the hatch cuts a diagonal line into the dim interior: dark one side, light the other. He is standing by the stove, a jar in his hand and a smile on his face.

'Coffee?' He asks, holding the jar towards her until it falls into the sun rays, the glass sparkling.

'Yes.' The port police will have to wait.

He puts a pan on the stove. The water from the bottle glugs into it in a rhythm, a rhythm that speeds up as the bottle empties and diminishes to a trickle with the last of the contents. He holds the empty bottle horizontally between his palms and crushes it, the sides concertinaing in, and then replaces the lid, which maintains the compression. Throwing it lightly into the air, he pops it off a contraction of his biceps. The balled bottle lands in the sink with the dirty dishes. This seems to amuse him and he smiles to himself as he turns the knob on the stove and the gas hisses. He then bends his knees to lower his sights to the level of the knobs, quickly turning the gas off again, as he does not seem to find whatever he is looking for.

'Where's the spark button?'

'You need matches.' Irini is still hanging through the hatch.

With a twist of his head to one side and a raise of his eyebrows, he asks why she isn't telling him where they are. It would be easier to show. With quick steps, she is below, the confined space bringing them close to each other. By reaching past him to the shelf where Captain Yorgos tucks the matches away, she rubs across his chest. The boat wallows and his hands are on her waist to steady her.

'Oh, there aren't any.' Irini pulls back and he lets go of her but their eyes lock. His bottom lip quivers. With the smallest of movements, his hand brushes her fringe from her eyes and then he breaks away.

'I'll get mine.' He is on deck and back before Irini can work out what just happened. He has his bag with him, a small dark green canvas rucksack, and from it he takes matches, strikes a light, and the gas hisses and ignites.

Irini tries to carry on as if nothing happened, but she finds she is distracted and her hands shake ever so slightly as she takes two cups down and finds a spoon. The sugar jar is empty and the milk in the fridge slops against the sides in lumps.

'Black then,' he says and sips through the steam.

'Sam, make a new life.' It is a beseeching request.

His face softens, a half-smile creates just one dimple.

'Please,' she adds.

He takes another sip of his drink and then puts it down on the saloon table.

'Any plastic bags on board?' he asks. It is an odd request but Irini pulls out a plastic carrier bag that is full of other plastic bags from under the sink. Yorgos keeps them there to line the rubbish bin.

'Will these do?' she asks. He takes them and puts his rucksack on the table. Flipping it open, he takes out a pair of balled socks and a pair of underpants. He puts them into a plastic bag and ties it securely.

Irini watches but says nothing as he waterproofs the rest of the contents. Is he agreeing to swim ashore, make a new life?

'Pass that pen.' He points to a biro rolling around on the chart table. Irini does as she is bid, but he just lays it to one side and continues bagging his possessions. There is a hardback book and a thin notebook.

'Does his mean you are going to do it then? Start again?'

'It means I like to be prepared.'

But as he delves deeper into his sack, he says, 'See if they are getting closer. Stay up there and watch.'

Irini understands she is being asked to leave, that there are things in his sack that he doesn't want her to see. She is glad to go on deck. If he doesn't want her to see something, then she does not want to see it. His world scares her.

The boats that are following have edged closer still. The land on the left is falling away; they have come to the channel that leads to Orino Island. Another hour would see them in Orino harbour. Maybe she should persuade him to turn here, go in close to the land so he can slip onto the island. So much of it is uninhabited, he could lay low for a while and then start again from there. What law has he broken anyway? Mercenaries are legal. He says he is wanted, but for what, and how much of it was his fault? She was a thief – every day - when she was homeless. Life pushed her to that to stay alive. What has life pushed him into?

If he has done wrong and they put him in prison, what incentive, when he gets out, will he have to start again? A criminal record won't help. He will come out penniless and with no future. He is bound to end up back in Casablanca, back to his old haunts. It is the only way he knows how to make money, to live life.

She swallows hard.

'Sam.' She looks down through the hatch. He has the first aid box out on the saloon table next to him and is writing in his notebook. He puts it down quickly as she calls.

'I just wanted to let you know that we are at the place where we would need to turn to go to Orino Island. It might be a good place to slip off, you know, hide low, think about a new life.'

His smile is broad and reassuring.

'What are the port police doing?'

'They have moved in a little closer.'

He nods. 'Okay. I'll be up in a moment.'

'Shall I change course?'

'No.'

Irini sits again and watches the boats behind, the channel opening out and the mainland passing by on the starboard side.

Something feels different. She is not sure if it is Sam's actions of waterproofing the contents of his rucksack or the closing in of the following boats.

As the last of the mainland slides away on the port side and the channel to Orino Island takes its place, the clouds touching the water there are all but black. If they sail that way, it looks almost sure that they will hit bad weather. The sea will grow dark and become choppy; the rain will obscure visibility. It might even be to Sam's advantage.

'Sam,' she calls down again. The saloon table is empty, the rucksack is over his shoulder. He has put his t-shirt back on but still has on his shorts. He looks ready to leave. It takes her by surprise. They have been motoring along together for six or seven hours now, and the thought of him suddenly not being there jerks at her. She has so much more to say to him, so much more she needs to listen to. They have only just begun. It is too soon.

'What?' he asks.

'Oh, I was just thinking that the weather over the island looks bad. It is bound to start raining over there soon. It will make visibility bad. Might be a good chance to get away.' His return smile is so warm, light, as if he does not have a care in the world.

'Seriously, it would be better than the calm weather straight ahead.'

'I have not made any decision yet.'

She steps back and sits down as he comes on deck. He stays low and slides onto the seat.

'Getting brave,' he comments as he sees how much the distance has closed between them and the port police boats.

'Why don't they just come alongside and arrest you? I mean, what difference does it make how slowly they come in? If that is their plan, I don't understand their hesitation.' Catching the darkness that crosses his face, she adds, 'Not that I want them to arrest you, but you can see what I am saying yes?'

'They know what they are doing,' he replies. 'They wait, they wait some more, they wait again. It is a game. I might make a slip-up, I might get fidgety. They will wait until either I or the dusk gives them the advantage.'

'What advantage will the dusk give them?'

'The same as the storm. Poor visibility can be turned to be either side's advantage.' He is looking at her with such concentration that she shifts her position, sweeps her fringe from her eyes. 'As long as the sky is blue and the waters are still, then nothing will happen. Which, for now, I would prefer.' He locks eyes with her. The implication is that he prefers it so he can sit and stare at her.

'Sam, do you think our memories will ever fade enough to live life like other people?'

'I think yours will.'

'Why, because yours include the child?' She is about to tell him how she is not sure that he is to blame for being so brainwashed but he speaks first.

'No, because you have the advantage of being loved and love can heal many wounds.'

'But if you make the decision to start a new life?'

He lets out a little laugh.

'Sam, it is possible.' She reaches out to him.

He takes her hand and looks at it, turning it over, stroking her palm with his other hand, and then he raises it to his lips and kisses the mound by the thumb, gently, as if she was a child sleeping.

'It's alright, Irini.' He wipes a tear from her cheek, tucking in his little finger so his loose skin does not touch her.

'No. It's not. It's very wrong. Please tell me that we will make a new life.'

Looking over the stern, he takes in air. His chest lifts as it fills and then collapses as he breathes out.

'Alright, Irini. When the light begins to fade.'

The relief she feels is dramatic.

Chapter 17

She is just not worth the effort. He has been
nothing but friendly and she has just left him
there, whilst he was struggling for breath,
coughing. How unkind was that?
The captain bends his knees and then his back,
slowly, in stages, as he reaches for his hat. It fell
to the ground in his coughing fit.
'You alright, old man?' A teenager passing by
stops and, with a graceful sweep of his arm and
a supple bow to his spine, he picks the captain's
cap up before the 'old man' can reach it. He
hands it back to him with a smile, the carefree
expression of youth.
'Who are you calling an old man?' Yorgos snaps.
'No offence meant.' And before Yorgos can
answer, the youth is gone, with long strides,
each of which has a slight bounce. The captain
shuffles his own feet forward.
Is that how the world sees him now, an old man?
Is that how he looks to other people? Sure, his

legs hurt and he struggles to walk at the moment, but everyone can have a temporary setback. They will come right. Although what the doctor could do next for him, he is not sure.

'Maybe I should have walked more,' he mumbles. 'Well, I am walking now; what more can I do?' He can feel a pressure in his sunburnt cheeks that he recognises as anger, but he has no idea who or what he is angry at. 'To hell with them all,' he mutters and his shuffles become a little more like a stomp, each foot padding down hard before lifting the next.

Before he is even at the bottom of the port police stairs, he can hear the commotion.

'But Irini is on board. How can you take that sort of risk?'

'I am not saying we will. We just have orders that they need to be prepared for it.'

'That is the same as saying they have permission to!'

It is Commander Demosthenes and Petta. Yorgos mounts the stairs, pressing his legs to move more quickly. Everyone in the room is gathered around the radio.

'What's going on?' Yorgos asks the nearest white-shirted youth as he spies Marina sitting by the radio operator, sobbing. It is pitiful sight, and he wonders if his earlier judgement was a bit harsh. His little legs gain momentum as he crosses the room to put a consoling arm around her, leaving the boy before he has had a chance to answer.

'What is going on?' he repeats, addressing anyone who will listen. No one does.

'That is the same thing,' Petta is shouting at Commandeer Demosthenes, his gentle eyes afire, spittle on his bottom lip. It is scary sight to see such a big man so angry.

'They are orders. What do you want me to do, risk my men? This pirate has a weapon of his own. You think he will not use it if he feels under threat?'

'That is my point. You tell your men to be armed and ready and he will feel threatened. Who wouldn't? Do you not understand? My wife is on board!'

Stroking across Marina's shoulders is very comforting; she is soft and the material of her dress is satin or silk, something smooth. Every second stroke, he lets his hand steer off course, touching the bare skin of her fleshy neck.

'I know, Petta. I know.' Demosthenes is doing his best to calm the man. 'Look, if, and God forbid that this should happen, but if he uses her, then we want to be ready.'

'Uses her?' Tears are running out of the corners of Petta's eyes but he pays them no heed. They course down the sides of his face and drip onto his shirt.

'It's possible,' the commander says.

'You mean, like as a shield or a hostage or something?' The colour has drained from Petta's face and Marina starts sobbing again. All attempts to either be quiet or ladylike seem to be forgotten. Yorgos takes a serviette from between the cup and saucer of an abandoned coffee. He offers it to Marina, who takes it without a thank you and blows her nose loudly.

Then a thought occurs to him and his hand drops from Marina's shoulder.

'Are you saying the port police might shoot at my boat?'

Petta's glare is hard and cold. Marina stops sniffing.

'It's possible.' The commander looks at the floor as he speaks.

'That is my home, my livelihood.' He can feel a pulse in his temple. Petta starts to speak again; Marina begins to say something. The radio crackles.

'Everyone calm down,' Commander Demosthenes says and picks up the microphone and listens.

'This is Port Police 1579, come in. Over.'
'1579, what is your position? Over.' The commander speaks clearly.
'We are closing in on him, both in position and armed. Over.'
'The orders from Athens are to take the opportunity when it arises, 1579. No need to wait for dusk. Over.'
'Understood. What about the girl? Over.'
'The girl is the opportunity. As soon as we contact her, that is your cue. Over.'
'Understood. Over and out.'

The line crackles again and goes quiet. Petta's mouth opens and closes like a drowning fish. Marina snivels into her hanky, and no one seems to have given one thought to his boat.

'So no one moves until you get in touch with Rini?' Petta asks, his voice quiet now.

'That's how it has to be,' the commander says. Marina's head lifts, her face blotchy from crying, but even so, there is something he just cannot help but like about the woman. Petta has stopped bristling and the tension in the room seems to have reduced. It gives a lull in the conversation.

'So if you hit my boat with bullet, I presume you will take responsibility for that and pay for the repair?' It is a reasonable question, and he is not shouting. That will help to calm everyone.

It seems as if the whole room turns to stare at him at once. Maybe they are looking at Marina? No, it is definitely him. His hand goes to his trouser zip, only to find it is done up. The commander is looking at him with disbelief. And then, as if they are of one mind, they turn away from him. The pulse in his temple becomes visible. His face becomes ashen and his eyes fill with tears.

'Oh, I am not saying that the boat is as important as...' But he is too late. No one is listening. Surely they cannot think that he was putting his boat before the girl? What must Marina think of him? He puts his hand back on her shoulder to stroke her again but she shrugs him off.

'*Artemis*, this is the port police. Over.'

They wait. Nothing but crackle.

'*Artemis*, are you there? Over?'

Chapter 18

The coffee lifts Irini and she feels a sense of happiness knowing that Sam will be starting his new life soon. She would like to know how he does. Maybe, when all this has died down, she can even be of some assistance to him. She looks over the stern of the boat.

Sam is lying on the cockpit seat, his legs up on the deck under the boom, his eyes closed – but he is not sleeping. She can tell somehow.

'Irini, would you do something for me?'

'Sure.' Anything to help.

'Sit here, next to me.'

Irini hesitates. He is indicating with a lazy finger the floor of the cockpit next to his seat. There is no reason why not; one bit of decking is much like another. She slips off her seat onto the floor and shuffles over, and turning her back on him, she puts her legs up onto where she has just been sitting. To her knowledge, he does not open his eyes.

The boat rocks and bobs its way along and the sun plays on her face as the boom swings in a small arc back and forth, blocking the sun, revealing the sun, blocking the sun. Her eyes reflex, opening and shutting in time with it. The blue sky, the red of her eyelids, the blue sky. Dark, light.

His touch is so gentle, she hardly feels it. By the time she is aware, it almost seems rude to stop him. His fingers gently stroke her hair, unobtrusive, respectful. It reminds her of Angelos stroking one of the many stray cats they feed, his touch so frightened of hurting, overcompensating by hardly touching at all. Her eyes close. Bright pink, deep red. The boom swings, the light changes.

The minutes stretch out. Time passes in a sun-soaked dream, neither sleeping nor wakeful. His hand grows more sure, but also more tender. The deck is hard and Irini leans her weight onto one hip and turns, her legs dropping from the seat, swivelling round, parallel with his, her head leaning against her arm, the elbow of which is on the seat next to him. Time seems to have stood still; there is nothing but the rocking and the pink on her eyelids. Her arm slips from its rest, her head rolls onto the seat, resting against his thigh, his hand stroking her hair that falls into the curve of her neck. The waves are never even, side to side, front to back, side to back, front to side, the yacht's movement never steady, never a constant; it lulls but it also jars.

An expected side roll becomes a lurch. Irini's drift into sleep is broken. She squirms to find a more comfortable position. Sam does the same. One of his legs drops to the floor and he slides with it, behind Irini, her upper body and head against his chest, his arms around her. The hardness of the floor, the half sleep, the uncertainty of the future time travels her back and she is trying to sleep the night she saw the little boy die.

She has walked for so long, trying to convince herself that life is worth living, that some day it will all make sense, that she has a future. She met up with another street child; she didn't even know his name. He was older than her but just as lost, and they walked together silently, neither asking each other what was the cause of their plight until cold and exhaustion took them to the back of a shop, a doorway, a place out of sight and they held each other with no words.

Just hugging, the warmth of the other reassuring until they fell asleep and then the dawn came and they rose and they walked away from each other, still with no names, still with no reason, still with no future but in that night, just the beat of each other's hearts had been enough to keep them going.

As she lays against his chest, she can hear the beat of his heart, so strong, such life, such power and with each beat a breath, his powerful lungs serving oxygen through his veins, bringing power to his muscles so he can hold her.

She has no idea if a minute has passed or several hours. The arch of the sun tells her it must be hours. The coffee from earlier brings the need for the toilet. She has no desire to get up but her bladder urges her. She shifts, and his grip tightens. She lifts his arm to break free and he kisses the top of her head and lets her go. She walks in a dream, the heat and the movement of the boat, the dreams and reality merging into one and, half-awake, she stumbles down into the cabin.

'*Artemis*, come in please. Over.' The radio sounds urgent, as if it has been calling for hours. She is still too soporific to care; the bathroom is more urgent. Sam has not put the first aid box back properly, but that too can wait. One of its corners is wedged in the sink; it is not going anywhere. She uses the toilet and comes to. The radio is still calling. Reality returns and she hears the urgency of the voice and responds to it.

'*Artemis*, are you there? Over.'

'*Artemis* here. Over.'

'Everything calm? Over.'

'Yes, everything calm. Over.' She looks up through the hatch but all she can see is one of Sam's feet.

'Rini, we need you to do something for us. Over.'

'What is it? Over.' Maybe if she can help, if they mean to arrest him, she could plead his case, help them understand. Maybe if they intend to do anything before dusk, she can put them off.

'Irini. Stay below deck. Over.'

'What?' She does not understand the message and she forgets to say 'over' before releasing the button.

'Stay below deck. Copy, do you hear? Over.'

181

'I hear but...' Irini looks back to the hatch where Sam's foot is no longer visible. She puts down the microphone and immediately there is a buzz and then the strangest cracking, splintering sound by her head and a hole appears in the woodwork by the radio.

Another buzz, more of a whizz and with a *thwack*, another hole appears. Her instincts spiral her on the floor.

'Sam, Sam! They are shooting.' There is the sound of his feet on deck, running.

'Sam, come below.'

His head appears in the hatch. His eyes are wide and dark, his colour flushed. For a fleeting second, he looks into her eyes and a smile begins to form, but there is no time.

'Stay below,' he mutters and is gone.

Crawling across the floor, Irini hears more pings and twangs of bullets hitting metal and wood. She pulls herself under the chart table and wraps herself around its single wooden leg. The port police never warned her. They didn't wait till dusk. He is so exposed up there. He must surrender.

'Sam, surrender!' she shouts at the top of her voice and then she hears a splash through the hull wall. He has dived in, he will have to swim fast, or under the water. He could stay hidden by the hull. If she goes on deck, she could distract the port police, wave her arms, or make out she is hurt. Anything to give him time to get away. The twanging and splintering has stopped as quickly as it started and

Irini quickly uncurls and extracts herself and makes for the steps.

The light outside is so bright. Without seeing anything, she waves her hands over her head.

'Here,' she shouts. 'Here.' How long will he need to swim to shore? Much longer than she can distract them. What else could she do?

Her eyes adjust and she sees that the police boats are all but alongside, one either side of the yacht. Men in bulletproof vests hold their rifles with the barrels pointing to the floor, their arms relaxed. No sign of tension.

He must be out of range. Five policemen line the deck of one boat and there are six on the other, all staring in the same direction, the same direction the splash came from. Irini steps up from the cockpit, onto the deck to follow their line of vision, to wish a secret good luck, but as she comes to the bows of *Artemis*, she stops.

Ballooned in the water is a grey t-shirt. How could he have taken it off whilst swimming to get away? The waves surge and on one side of the t-shirt, something brown surfaces. But his rucksack was green.

One of the port police has a boat hook. He leans over the pulpit of his boat and reaches for the balloon. With a poke and a pull, he moves it through the water. A wave takes it from his grasp. It turns. Sam's face beneath the waves. Green eyes staring. Mouth open.

She can hear radio talk from the police boat. 'Crackle. Over. Copy. Crackle.' Two of the port police put their free arms in the air and cheer. One slaps the other on the back and they turn away. Irini's ears ring.

'Irini, Irini?' Someone is shaking her by the shoulder. She doesn't hold back her reaction, hitting the hand away. 'Easy, easy. You are okay now. You are safe.'

The speaker's eyes are brown. He is wearing a bulletproof vest, but he has no gun.

'You want to go across to the police boat? Here, I can help you.' He lifts his leg, straddling the two rails. The boats are alongside. 'Here, give me your hand.'

Irini turns away from him, looks back at the balloon of grey t-shirt in the water. It has arms now, laid outwards as if crucified. His head has rolled back in the water so only his Adam's apple is visible. Some of the bandaging she carefully bound around his wound has come loose and trails from under the t-shirt like tentacles.

'Okay, get him out,' someone orders. But he is silenced by another who points to her. Some distance away from his body floats his rucksack. A boat hook from the police boat on her other side grabs for it, and it is upended on the deck.

'Just clothes in bags,' someone calls.

'Irini, you are safe now. Come.' The man closest to her is still urging and reaches out, one leg on the police boat and one on the yacht. Lashing out at his arm, she pads to the hatch and steps down into the relative dark.

Above her are the sounds of many feet now. Words drift to her. 'Shock' is one of them. Someone suggests, 'Give her time.' Another, 'Give her space.' Someone uses the word *ordeal*. Another says, 'Keep an eye on her.' She slumps onto one of the padded saloon seats. His coffee cup is still there, half-drunk but completely cold. She puts her hands where his have been, holds the mug, squeezing it tightly until with a sudden spring, she leaps to her feet and throws it with all her force into the pile of washing up in the sink. From the back of her throat comes a primordial growl as the kettle rocks and falls to the floor. A head dips through the hatch but with one glare from Irini, they retreat.

'Right, there's enough fuel. You two sail her back. We're staying close. Any change in the girl and we stop, put her on the radio to her man as soon as she has calmed down. Get her connected back to her own life. But give her time if that is what she needs. I have a wife the same: all emotion and highly strung. Best just give her time.' Voices are very easy to hear on deck when no motor is running. The motor starts up and Irini is glad she can no longer hear their inane talk.

She lays down on the saloon bench and as the boat begins to move, it is not long before she is overcome by sleep.

A light shake awakes her.

185

'You want coffee?' The policeman is about the same age as Sam.

She shakes her head.

'Shall we radio in so you can talk to your husband?'

His tone is kind; he means well.

She shakes her head again.

'Are you sure?' He is genuinely surprised.

Irini squirms and turns away, putting her face into the back of the saloon seat.

She can hear him breathing over her and then he is gone. Sleep is the best refuge.

'*Artemis* here. Over.'

'How is Irini? Her husband is here. He wants to speak to her. Over.'

'I think she is asleep. Over.'

'He says leave her to sleep. Over.'

When she wakes, there is a cup of orange juice on the table next to her. She drinks it with greed and drifts back to sleep.

The sound of liquid being poured brings her out of a dreamless sleep. The light outside is not so bright. The port policeman puts the cup of orange juice by her without a word. He looks at her but she looks away.

Her face feels crumpled and sticky. The confined space in the toilet is also a pull. There is so little room that she rarely pulls the door to when using the bathroom, but on this occasion, she does. Pulls it closed and locks it. Reducing her world. Shutting everything out. Closing herself in.

Putting the seat down, she sits. The enclosed space brings some relief. The door is a hand span from her face so sitting down, she can lean her forehead on it. The towel has fallen from its hook and a corner of it is below the duckboard and in the water that swims around under it. She will swill her face.

The first aid box is half in the sink. The lid is not properly closed again and she recalls it being on the saloon table with Sam. She lifts it with care and puts it on the toilet seat, swills her face, and sits again, the water dripping into her lap where she holds the first aid box.

When she took the bandage from the box, he was alive. When he had it with him on the saloon table, he was alive, too. The edges dig in where she hugs it to her chest but the pain feels appropriate. The tears begin to fall. Her chest heaves and her whole body convulses. With her nose running, she struggles to breathe and her breath comes in big gasps as she pulls handfuls of tissues and tries to blow her nose before another wave of tears consumes her. The depth of her loss hollows out her chest and leaves a gaping, empty space. With her tears for him come tears for herself, tears for the hardships she endured as a homeless teenager and the horrors she has seen, the empty black nights of no sleep, the fights over scraps of food and pieces of bedding, her lungs tearing for air after running from store holders she has stolen from and pimps who wanted to use her.

She cries for the ugliness of life she has been forced to see and the unfairness of the shallow lives enjoyed by the people who have not seen that life she has led, the life that runs parallel to all civilisation. She cries until she is exhausted and her head once more touches the door. The towel is soaking up the bilge water and next to it is an antiseptic cream that belongs in the first aid box.

'*Artemis*, are you there? Over.'

Irini has no idea how long they have been calling.

Chapter 19

It is strange how, in a mist of excruciating emotional pain, part of her brain continues to function as normal. What does it matter that the antiseptic cream is on the floor? There is a man dead and bullet holes in the boat. But the antiseptic cream should not be on the floor. Her hand mechanically reaches for the tube, the first aid box digging deeper into her ribs. The tube scoots from the ends of her fingers and requires a second, more purposeful lurch to secure it.

'Got you,' Irini says out loud and she grimly marvels all over again that words can still be formed and tasks can still be carried out even when unspeakable things have happened that are so momentous they reduce the mundane to irrelevant.

The tube has been used and around the top, dried cream creates a crusty rim around the lid. She peels off the top of the first aid box to put it away.

Bandages do not spring for freedom, medicinal smells do not fill the small room. The box has been filled with something that has been neatly stored with a plastic bag around it, and on top is a notebook.

Sam's notebook.

The one he was writing in while in the saloon.

Before he died.

The tears burst their temporary dam again and the box trembles on her knee as she clutches the book to her chest. This time, she cries for the obscene and purposeless waste of his life. He would have surrendered. He could have started a new life.

'You all right, Miss?' The words accompany a knock on the door.

'Fine.' She responds quicker than she would have expected she was able. Reflexes take over. Holding her breath to stop the tears, she listens.

'Crying. Best leave her be,' the tapper says.

'Not far from port now,' another answers.

And then a noise somewhere between a grunt and a sigh and footsteps retreat and rap quickly up on deck and there is silence.

Holding her breath has stopped the tears and she strokes the outside cover of the notebook before opening it to the first page.

There is a drawing of a mouse, delicate and sensitive, a smaller study of one of its feet below it and several attempts at its tail.

She turns the page.

Another mouse and a study of an open tin can with a very jagged edge, as if it has been opened with a knife, or torn open, perhaps.

The next page. A shelter, sticks leaning against a fallen tree, leaves and branches over the top, inside of which is another can and a pair of boots.

She turns each page over, slowly taking in the loneliness of his life, the hardship he has endured. One study covers two pages. It is a room without curtains at the window. There is a single bed and a chair, the same pair of boots, another can, and a big knife. It is like the shelter but inside. There is no adornment, no pictures on the wall, no television, nowhere to sit, bare. But the shocking factor is that through the window is what looks to be a panorama of a city, with flat-topped houses, palm trees, modern skyscrapers, and minarets piercing the skyline. Casablanca? It could be, but she is not sure. It is some place of civilisation anyway, but the room is far from any of civilisation's comforts.

At the bottom of this page in curly writing is a single word: Home.

The heaviness in her chest swells, rises, sticks in her throat and the tears roll again, but this time in quiet sobs.

She turns the page.

'Dear Rini,'

Her tears are instantly dried. His voice is in her head and she is still. It takes a moment to blink the saline away so she can see, a moment to gather her courage to read on.

You are sitting on deck as I am writing this. The sun outside, bouncing off the water, is creating wavy

191

shadows and light on the ceiling down here and it would be lovely to continue to make believe that we are on some watery holiday.'

Irini rubs the back of her hand across her eyes to clear her vision.

Unfortunately, that is not true and if you are reading this then, as my friend once said, 'Job Done.' I didn't understand what he meant at the time, but I do now.

The moment I boarded this yacht, I knew that there was only one of two ways it could go. Either I would sail without incident to Casablanca, ignored by all, or, as the sitting duck I am, it will be my coffin.

I knew the moment I saw the two tiny dots leaving Saros after we had made some way from port that it was to be my watery grave. Knowing I have nothing left but a few hours, all I want to do, in this few hours, is to pretend life is normal, that you are my wife or girlfriend or even just my friend or something and that this is a holiday. What else have I left? Nothing? All I have is a few hours on a sailing boat. I have no choice about the length of time I have to live, nor a change of scenery in which to spend that time. All I have is the choice of how I choose to see it. So I choose to see the beauty of the blue sky, the magnificence of the brilliance of the sun, the hypnotic fascination of the sea and the deep beauty of the person I am with.

I am so glad it is you, Irini, that I am spending final hours with. If it had been someone who had led nothing but a 'normal' life, how would that person ever be able to relate to me, let alone understand me? The breadth of your experience has given you a compassion that breaks past immediate wrongdoing to see the person and their life as a whole and I could not have been given a greater blessing than to have spent this time with you.

You have given me such warmth, Irini. It is as I imagine love to be. You reached across and touched me with love and showed me how it could be.

Which in a way makes the outcome that is inevitable even sadder, but also, and oddly at the same time, it makes it easier.

I knew the risks when I chose the boat. I really didn't have much hope of reaching Casablanca either by land or sea, but as I sit here now, I am pretty sure that I don't, or should I say, didn't, really want to.

Casablanca is just the start of the same old cycle. Another contract, another war, more dead or injured, more threats and fears. I can honestly say I have had enough of life. My head is too full of things no one should ever see, and once you know a thing, you cannot unknow it. So my guess is a part of me chose the boat to avoid death in some concrete, crumbling corner. If I have to die, then let it be here, under the sun, surrounded by the beauty of the sea and, with a touch of good fortune, with warm and loving company I have had the luck to find in you.

So you see the words 'Job done' fit and I now know what my friend meant when he said them. Suicide does not always have to be by your own hand.

If I read what I have written over, I will start to make changes and get hung up on it not being perfect, so I will not read it over, Irini. You get it straight from my heart in its raw state. If I find after my death that somehow we get another chance, I shall ask to wait so next time *around I can be deployed with you. With someone like you close by in the early years, my life would have been so different.*

So a million thanks, Irini, just for being you. Never wish to lose the things that happened to you because these are the things that make you who you are. A person who can listen without judging, care without stipulations. A compassionate, warm, loving, and wholly decent person. Not many who claim that have the right to do so, but you do, Irini. You really do.

I think what I feel for you is love. I certainly have never felt such a feeling before so I will sign off 'with love' and mean it with all my being. Would it be misplaced to ask you to always keep a little piece of me in your heart so I know I live on? A part of me is afraid of this big choice I have made and it gives me comfort to think that even the smallest part of me might stay with you, tucked away in the warmth of your compassion.

That's it. If I say any more I will be repeating myself.

Thank you a thousand times over.

Do not cry for me, as this was my choice.

With love,

Peter. (Sam :))

His name was Peter. The mercenary who had no mother, who was unloved by his father, who was too sensitive to be a soldier. Peter.

Irini compresses all her feeling for him, all the unfairness that was his life, all the understanding he gave her, all the mutual experiences they have had that created their connection together, down into a tiny cushion of beauty which she tucks away in her heart.

She turns the page almost as an automatic reflex.

P.S. The bandages and Iodine and things are on the bed in the rear cabin (Not the Captain's).

This makes Irini look again at the first aid box. Whatever is wrapped in layers of plastic bags fits the box well.

What is in the bag is yours. Do not tell them about it or they will take it from you, and I can see no good that will do.

P.P.S It is not dirty.

Putting the notebook carefully by the sink, Irini feels the plastic bag item. It has some give but it is not soft. As she slides her hand down the side between plastic and box, she tries to lift it out as a whole, but it begins to fall into pieces inside the bag. The carrier handle is folded underneath and pulling this up, she can open it.

She gasps and stares.

Looking back at the open notebook, she re-reads the P.P.S. before putting her hand in to lift out a bundle of fifty euro notes. Underneath is another bundle with Arabic writing on it, and a stack of British fifty pound notes, a wedge of notes with what looks like Russian or Rumanian writing on them, and a bundle that looks clean and pressed with Scandinavian writing perhaps. She has no idea what all the different currencies are. All she knows is that it is a lot.

'Miss?' There is a tap on the door. 'Miss, we are coming into harbour.' The footsteps march away waiting for no answer.

She has to choose and choose quickly. He says it is not dirty. What does that mean? Is it his pay? If it is, does she feel that it is dirty? But he said that as a mercenary, he did not clear houses, that they only defended. How had he put it? 'Defend person or post.' Mercenaries are legal, right? So this is legal pay. Besides, what would the port police do with it? Would it get sunk in their coffers or go to the government, where it would slip into back pockets? She certainly doubts it would be used to do any good.

Folding the bag over the notes again, she returns the whole to the box, puts the notebook on top, strokes the cover, the words within, and snaps the lid back on.

The engine revs slow to idle. They no longer seem to be moving.

She unlocks the door.

Chapter 20

Irini will not be helped up the steps onto the deck. Outside is no longer bright; rather, there is a softening to all the lighter colours, the whitewashed buildings, the cream tops of tables outside the cafés all touched pinkish in the twilight that turns the deepest greys to blues and the blacks to purples.

Standing on the quay side at the other end of the homemade gangplank, lined up, are Petta and Marina, Angelos holding their hands between them, Captain Yorgos, and Commander Demosthenes, whom she only just recognises. The mayor is there, along with several of his sidekicks, and two lawyers. The younger one she recognises as Babis, who lives in her village, and held back by the port police are teams of television cameras and reporters. They surge forward as they see her, shouting her name.

Her throat feels a little sore when she swallows and her ears are ringing.

'Irini, over here. Rini.'

'Look here, Irini.'

A hundred flashes fire with a quick succession of clicks.

Irini's grip on the rail and the box against her chest tightens. One of the port police offers her his hand but she ignores it.

Angelos is trying to pull free of Petta and Marina's grip, but they both hold on. All thoughts leave Irini as she runs across the gangplank and, thrusting the first aid box at Petta, she picks up her little boy. Her nose sinks into his neck and she takes a deep breath before tucking his head under her own chin. A big arm comes around her and she is about to duck from under it when she realises it is Petta. He pulls her to him firmly, his arms around both of them. Over the top of his shoulder, she can see that Marina is now holding the box. She swallows. It hurts.

Marina gives the impression that she is reading the words on the box top: 'Artemis, First Aid' in faded felt pen on the lid. Marina turns to Captain Yorgos, who is standing open-mouthed, gaping at his yacht. She offers the box to him and he takes it, but his eyes do not leave his Artemis. Irini breaks free of Petta but cannot grab the box, as she has Angelos in her arms. She hands him to Petta.

'What have you done to my boat!' Captain Yorgos exclaims. He thrusts the first aid container into the hands of the nearest port police so he can hold on as he goes aboard. Irini pushes through the mayor's group of people to get to the box.

'What have you done?' the yacht captain repeats. The teams of photographers turn their attention from Irini to the boat. Petta is trying to pull

Irini back, keep her safe, but she is watching the progress of the box, her hand on her throat, controlling her breathing.

'Is that a bullet hole?' Someone points. This creates a buzz. A little scuffle breaks out. The camera crews try again to push past the port police. They begin to surge and Commander Demosthenes beckons the officers around the gangplank and on the police boat to come and help with the crowds.

The port policeman with the first aid box hands it to one of the policemen getting off the boat. He is one of the snipers and wears a bulletproof vest. He in turn looks for somewhere to leave the box and, in passing, puts it in an orange crate that has been tied onto the back of one of a line of mopeds to serve as a basket. Irini watches, relieved that no one seems to take any notice of it.

'Come on. I will take you home.' Petta's arms do not release her and he carries Angelos. Marina is grinning and crying into a handkerchief with black butterflies embroidered on it as she follows them. Irini struggles to get to the box and, thankfully, Petta seems to be steering her in the same direction. Her throat is getting sorer by the minute. It seems unlikely that she is getting a summer cold, as she has never had one before, but it is possible. Behind them, the crowds are becoming uncontrollable and Captain Yorgos can be heard shouting.

'Get off my boat. You cannot board without my permission! I am the captain. Get off!'

They are nearly next to the bike. Another few steps and Irini will have the box safely back in her arms again. Petta hands Angelos back to her and her attention is taken by him. She is also having trouble fully closing her mouth. If her teeth are together, it puts pressure on the glands under her ears. Angelos smells sweet, his eyelashes are even longer than she remembers them, his cherub mouth so perfect. She kisses him all over his face, glad to be reunited, and he rewards her with a big smile, reaching out to touch her face in return.

'Do you feel up to driving, Mama?' Petta asks Marina. Irini is all absorbed with the love she is feeling, the joy of being together with her life's blood, the relief at not being dead. 'Irini, you and Angelos go in the car with Mama.' He looks into her eyes as he speaks. 'Let's get away from this madness.'

Irini looks around. She has moved a few steps whilst thinking of nothing but her son, and they have passed the bike. She looks back. She has a headache coming on. The photographers and television teams surround the bike, trying to get to the boat. It gets pushed over. Irini makes a move toward it but Petta is firm in keeping her moving toward the car. Someone who is watching the spectacle by the boat, who has no microphone or camera, rights the bike. A man with a hairy microphone picks up the box, presses the lid down firmly, and puts it back in the orange crate before continuing his jostling to get on the boat.

One of the anchormen, suited and smart, sits sidesaddle on the bike, his crew filming him as he gives what must be a progress report to the camera that is focused on him.

'Petta, will you go and get that box that's in the back of that bike there?' Irini asks, each word rasping on her throat. Her forehead feels hot.

'Let's just get you away. It'll be fine there.' Petta puts his hand on her forehead. He is crying. 'You feel a bit hot. You alright?'

A van pulls up and a new group of reporters descends onto the scene. As some of the original reporters turn to see who the new crew is by the logo on the side of their van, they spot Irini and Petta trying to leave.

Irini sees their intention and hurries to the car.

'Irini, did he hurt you?'

'Irini, did he threaten you?'

'Did he use you as a human shield?'

'Irini, are you glad to be alive?'

'Back off,' Petta growls and he ushers Irini and Angelos into the car. Another group of photographers breaks off from the group by the boat and they come running in hopes that they will get better results from Irini than they are getting from the port police, Yorgos, and the boat.

Petta is now pushing a cameraman away. 'Irini, stay in the car.'

'But there is something I need to get.' She can hardly talk. She swallows and it causes her pain. The last thing she needs is to be sick, but she is definitely coming down with something.

'What?' Petta almost shouts. He is distracted by putting his hand over a camera lens that has been thrust in through the car window.

'It's a box,' Irini begins but she does not want the reporter to hear.

'Marina, just drive. Go. Irini, we can get whatever it is later,' Petta says. The cameramen jump to one side as Marina drives at them.

'Wait.' Irini finds her voice. It sounds croaky and unreal. 'Marina, there is something I need you to go back and get.'

It is as if she has not spoken.

'Oh my love, I am so glad you are unharmed. Petta has not eaten a thing all day; he was beside himself with worry. Oh my dear child, it is such a relief you are back with us. Is Angelos all right there? Is he sleeping?'

'Marina, stop the car.'

Marina loses her smile and stops.

'I will wait here. I want you to go back and get the box out of the back of the bike that was standing by the boat.' The car seems to be moving even though they have stopped. She puts her hand on her forehead and can feel the heat.

'Box, bike? Irini, what bike? Do you mean boat? What are you saying? You have just escaped. We thought you might be dead. You are alive! Everything else can wait. Relax!' Marina stops to look at Irini and takes a breath. She puts her own hand on

202

Irini's forehead and a frown replaces her smile but she says, 'Everything is fine now. You are back. Your son has a mother. My son, your husband, has a wife. Everything is as it should be. Nothing is more important than that, is it?'

Irini hears her words and they sink in. She does not have the energy to argue. Besides, Marina is right. Thirteen or fourteen hours ago, she wondered if she was going to ever see her son or husband again. Thirteen or fourteen hours ago, a gun was thrust in her face and everything changed. The most important thing was her freedom. But six or seven hours ago, a man was shot and everything changed again. The most important thing is that she is alive.

No box, no matter what it contains, is as important as being back with Angelos and Petta. Where is Petta? Why did he not come in the car with them? She suddenly feels very tired and even answering her own question takes more effort than she has left. Every swallow emphasises how unwell she feels and she wonders if she will ever be well and energetic again.

'You must be hungry. Have you eaten anything at all today? I've nothing ready; been at the port police office all day. Not a moment to cook. I'll stop and get a chicken from Stella's,' Marina says. Irini loves the small eatery in the village that fills farmers' stomachs with grilled sausages and chicken with lemon sauce, chips, and ouzo, but right now, she is not sure if she could eat a thing.

As they enter the village, the eatery is lit up. The fairy lights wrapped round the tree in the middle of the tables on the pavement are inviting, and a group of farmers sit at one of the tables, a large plate of chicken, sausages, and chips in the middle. There is also a bottle of ouzo on the table, and they are picking hungrily at their meal. In one way, Irini is surprised that Stella is still there, carrying on, doing something as ordinary as cooking chicken and chips when in other places in the world people are being shot, their lives snuffed out. But of course it is still there; why would anything have changed since she left the village? It is she who has had her life changed.

She wipes sweat from her eyes. The night is warm but she is sweating as though she has a fever.

The car bumps to a stop. Stella comes out and runs toward them and, leaning through the open window, she kisses Irini firmly on each cheek.

'Oh how wonderful you are back. You feel a little hot; are you alright? I would not be surprised if you had a little fever after such an ordeal. But now you are home and we are all glad you are.' She has more to say but the ringing in Irini's ears drowns her out and it does not seem very important to listen to her. Stella's talking quickly exhausts her. Stella's husband Mitsos wanders out from the eatery at a leisurely pace, grins at Irini, and offers Marina two large silver foil boxes. Dinner is on him, he says, and he is glad Irini is back.

Leaning back against the car seat, Angelos curls up on her lap but it is only a couple of car lengths before Marina pulls the car to a stand in the square. The men in the kafenio must recognise the car as they begin to trickle out of their smoked-filled domain towards them. The lady from the kiosk, Vasso, comes out of her hut and the people in the pharmacy leave their tinctures and bandages behind and join them as they all crowd around the car, delighted to see Irini, hoping she is well, offering her coffee and chats when she is ready, pressing in on her, enclosing her, stifling her. With brisk but quiet thanks for their goodwill, she pushes though them, cradling Angelos, to the corner shop, through to the courtyard and up to her son's room, where she joins him on the floor with his favourite wooden train, making it go back and forth and round and round and she tries to ignore her pulsing forehead and her raw sore throat, tries to forget everything as she focuses on nothing but the sound of Angelos' giggles.

'Irini, wake up, *agapi mou*.' The heaviness that is Angelos is lifted off her.

'Irini, it might be best if you come and have a little to eat before bed.' His voice is coming from by the crib. He must be laying the sleeping boy down for the night. 'Rini?' His arms are around her, lifting her up. 'My love,' he says and pulls her head into his chest, wipes her fringe off her forehead, and kisses the top of her head, whispering, 'As if you have not been through enough in your life,' almost as if he is talking to himself.

He is so big and powerful compared to her slight frame that he could lift her and carry her as easily as she lifts and carries Angelos, but she would not like to be treated like a child and he knows it. He has a respect for her toughness, her independence.

She struggles to get to her feet. She has no energy left and her head is pounding. Petta's arms are still around her and he looks her in the eyes, his liquid brown eyes saying more than his words ever could, all his love openly displayed in them, all his care. His hand slides down to the back of her legs and he scoops her up without breaking contact and carries her from the room. He doesn't make her feel like a child. Instead, she feels loved, cherished, protected. He carries her down the stairs and out into the courtyard where Marina has put out plates on the table under the lemon tree. The sky is black now, smeared with the Milky Way, the moon haloed by its own glow. The wisteria scrapes gently against the wall as a cat rubs its cheeks against the stem. The jasmine perfumes the night. The warmth is a perfect temperature.

He lowers her into a chair and Marina serves her some chicken which she pours lemon sauce over and then heaps on chips.

They all sit and look at each other without speaking, everyone a little shocked by the normality of the meal after such an extreme day. Almost as if it is an agreement, they eat in silence and then Marina is left with the dishes as Petta carries Irini back up the stairs and slides her under the covers of their own bed, where he pulls her against him and holds her as sleep comes to them both.

Chapter 21

The cockerel crows and Irini is awake. It must be time to get up, go to clean Captain Yorgos' boat, make enough money to get through another day. The sun streams through the curtains where they do not meet the ceiling. Another thought unsettles her, turns her stomach. It is not fully formed and then her time with Sam and the police grappling hook on the ballooned t-shirt rush into her consciousness, causing her to groan. Her throat is still sore and her ears are still ringing.

Petta's big arm is around her, pulling her back under the covers. Curling side by side, he lifts his knees higher and tucks his head over her. She is encircled by him. It is so safe and warm and cosy, she would love to stay cuddled in his embrace, trusting that everything will be alright. But what happened to Sam does not alter their position in life and they still need the extra money she brings in to ensure they can keep paying the loan against the shop, put food on the table, or whichever way they divide up the income.

'Where are you going?' Petta asks, his voice rough with sleep.

'Work,' Irini says, her own voice cracking in response to the soreness in her throat, and she struggles to free herself. As the covers untwist from her legs, a second memory rushes her. Her limbs freeze as she remembers the box, Sam's – no, Peter's, she corrects herself – safety net. Why had she not hung onto it more tightly? What on earth possessed her? Trying to recall what happened feels like walking through glue. Yesterday has all the qualities of a dream, the sort where she runs and runs and gets nowhere, the sort where she finds herself back on the street at the age she is now and she isn't quite sure how she got there, the sort that wakes her in the early hours of the morning in a cold sweat and leaves her unable to go to sleep again.

She will use the cover of work to go and try to track down the box. If the authorities have it, she will put up a good argument as to why it is hers. The notebook with the drawings and the letter to her may be persuasive, even considered to be a will? If the authorities don't have it, then who has? Whose moped was it? It seemed familiar.

'Irini, *agapi mou*, there is no work today.' Petta nuzzles into the back of her head.

'It is another day and money needs to be earned.' She tries to move again. Her head throbs. Another groan escapes her rasping throat.

'Are you alright?' Petta's voice is alert now, concerned.

'I screwed up.' Irini lays lifeless until a wave of tension urges her into action. She would like to tell him about the money, the gift, but why give him a glimpse of how unstressed their lives could have been, just to snatch it away again? 'I'd best go,' she says.

'Irini, what happened yesterday was in no way your fault, you know, and there is no boat to clean this morning.' She half-turns to look at his face as he speaks.

'You think he will have sacked me?' Her eyes widen. If she cannot find the box, she will still need the job.

Petta smiles and places a gentle kiss on her unresponsive lips. 'Captain Yorgos will be strutting about demanding compensation for the bullet holes and the police will probably want to look over the boat to do whatever it is they do in the aftermath of such things. I don't think anyone is going to let you, or anyone else, go near the boat today.' He strokes her arm. His legs over-lock hers, trying to keep her close. 'The last thing you need is to go to the boat, or to go anywhere else today, for that matter. How are you feeling?' His puts his hand across her forehead.

'We have bills,' Irini begins.

'Shhh,' Petta whispers and kisses the back of her head. 'You worry too much.' But Irini cannot lay still. She kicks his legs off hers and she is up and dressed before Petta's feet are even on the floor. With a quick look in to check that Angelos is still sleeping, she trips lightly and quickly down the stairs and through the kitchen to sit, arms folded, under the lemon tree. Her phone is there, showing three missed calls and a message. All are from Stathoula. How could she so completely have forgotten about Stathoula?

With agile thumbs, the message appears.

There's been a delay. I have not left Germany yet. I tried to call but got no answer. I will try again.

Irini feels a relief from tension she did not know was there. She has not missed her. A tightness across her chest reminds her how much she wants to see Stathoula, but the desperate need to talk seems to have diminished now. It will be enough to hug her, drink coffee with her, be with her. Maybe if she can get things sorted today, there will be time for all that.

The relative cool of the early morning air under the lemon tree feels like it is helping her think. She needs to find the box and get it back.

The slap of Petta's feet resounds in the kitchen, followed by the creak of Marina's door. They try to talk quietly but she can hear them.

'It has probably opened old wounds,' Marina says. 'Reminded her of the uncertainty of life.'

'I want to make her feel safe,' Petta says, almost a whisper.

'Unfortunately, we are not in a position to do that. But maybe we can take more of the strain. She is not going to go back and work for that Captain Yorgos, for a start. He is a revolting little man. You need to find a job, or maybe I can get work in a hotel in Saros making beds or something.'

There is a tapping at the front door.

'Just a minute, Mama,' Petta says and his feet slap on the flags in the hallway to the door.

'*Kalimera?*' Irini can hear Theo's voice, the man who runs the kafenio. What would he want so early? The talk is low, but she hears her name mentioned, then Petta says *ah* as if he understands.

'But she is not going back there,' Petta insists.

'Is that anything to do with me?' Irini shouts.

'I was just explaining to Theo that you won't be going back to Captain Yorgos,' Petta soothes.

Irini is on her feet. 'Who are you to decide that!' She marches through the house to the front door, her head throbbing in response to each step. 'How can I help you, Theo?'

He is a man with a frizzy halo of hair and as he stands there, the halo, lit up in the early morning sun, is more appropriate than he knows. He is nothing short of an angel as far as Irini is concerned because in his hand is the first aid box.

'Hi Rini. Glad you are back on dry land.' He gives her a smile that expresses his relief. He is one of the many people who comes to the shop to talk to her, confide his secrets. 'Found this in the back of the bike after Petta borrowed it yesterday. Well, I wasn't sure what to do with it. It has the name *Artemis* on it, so I thought… but I can take it back to the boat if you are not going back.' He smiles again and begins to back away so as not to intrude.

Irini controls herself not to snatch, but once the box is in her arms, she closes the door perhaps slightly quicker than is polite and rushes past Petta and Marina and back to the table in the courtyard. She rips the lid off. The book lays on top. She grabs it and hugs it to her chest and closes her eyes, squeezing out the tears of renewed sadness for Sam, but also of relief.

'You alright?' Marina asks. She comes from the kitchen, a coffee cup in each hand.

Irini opens her eyes and with a shaking hand feels the plastic bag in the box. It is there, the bundles of notes, the escape from their struggle.

'Irini, what is it?' Petta reacts positively to Irini's animation. But she has no time to answer. Running into the kitchen, she takes the basket out from under the table with the coffee stove. It is heavy but not too heavy to be lugged out to the table beneath the lemon tree. With a quick movement, she upturns it and the bills and notices they have been struggling to meet fall out.

'What on earth?' Petta begins. Sifting through the papers, she puts all the most recent bills in a pile, the agreement for Marina's loan on top. It makes her cross just to see it. If she had been living here when the storm happened and the tree fell through the roof, she is pretty sure she could have found a loan with better terms. Some shark just took advantage of Marina. Her movements grow sharp with the anger it generates in her.

'Rini?' Petta asks again. But her mouth is set hard and without another word, she runs from the house with the box, grabbing a basket from the kitchen for the bills along the way, and with sweat of her breaking fever running down the sides of her face, heads for the car. It has always been her way to take action and tell people what she has done afterwards but this time, there is no way she is letting anyone know what she is doing first. She is not sure what Petta will say about the money. He may well claim it is dirty, even if it was legitimate pay. Well, she is not going to take that chance. Damn it, after all she has been through, life owes her!

Driving to Saros, the oranges trees speeding past, it is hard to believe that it was only twenty-four hours ago that she was making the same journey, completely unaware that the day's events would be taken out of her hands.

Today is different. Today she will control all the events in their lives. Her first stop is the bank. Much of what she intends to do today can be done there.

Chapter 22

Her instincts tell her to go to more than one bank to change all the foreign money, but in reality, as she goes to each teller, no one bats an eyelid. Someone waiting in one of the queues to be served makes a quip. Something about 'Has she been working abroad?' but she replies that she has a shop and there have been tourists, and this seems to satisfy their curiosity.

Relief is what she expects to feel as she pays off bill after bill. She pays the straightforward ones first; the water and electricity, a handful of cash and a stamp from the official and they are done. Then she goes to pay the outstanding TEVE, the social security contributions. She knew this would be exasperating. She is danced from one desk to another, trying to find the right paperwork and the right person. At one point, she wonders if they even want her money and feels inclined to leave but then the right person is found. Another handful of cash and a stamp and their insurance is up to date.

The last bill she goes to pay is the loan against the shop. For some reason, even paying this off feels like a heavy chore. The whole issue is so loaded with emotions, it is hard to distinguish appropriate feelings from imagined fears. But after finding the right office in the right building, the man could not be nicer and as she walks from the building, it hits her that her family is no longer in debt to anyone. With a huge exhale of air, a thousand knots seems to release from her back. Her brow, which she thought was relaxed, smooths flat and a bounce that has long been absent from her walk returns. The uppermost feeling is that of satisfaction.

And there is money left.

'Thank you, Sam,' she whispers into the air.

It crosses her mind to go to the main square in Saros to have a coffee in celebration and watch the people purposefully marching here and there in their morning work, but really, she wants to be back at the village. Back amongst the people who genuinely seem to care. To tell Petta that they can return to the carefree couple they were before they moved here.

She puts the basket, which just a few hours ago contained months of unpaid bills but now holds the plastic bag with the remaining money, on the passenger seat. It was the interest rates that were slowly crippling them. Each month, paying off the required amount was not enough, the total amount owed forever, silently, creeping upwards. But now, all that is gone.

Having parked by the harbour, the view in front of her is the sea, sparkling in a very similar way to the way it had sparkled yesterday, the same water, the same colour, the same waves. Irini stops and just looks.

Sam is dead. The man she knew so briefly has given her more security than she has ever felt in her life. She puts her hand on the plastic bag of the remaining money. There is still a lot left. The time she was with him was so short, she partly feels she never really met him at all, but another part of her cannot believe that she won't see him today and every day for the rest of her life. She would like to honour him somehow, but she has no idea about that sort of thing. She would like to tell Petta about him. In fact, she would like to tell Petta about all the things she has held back from him, the bits that show her in a bad light and the bits he cringes to hear. All of it, her whole life, and she would also like to tell him how Sam made her feel and how, for that, she loved him.

No, perhaps not that last bit. She half-closes her eyes to see as far as she can across the sea. He chose his death. She must not forget that. It was what he wanted. Sort of. Seeing as he could not erase his memories.

There is a tap on her window and she jumps. With the sun behind them, it is difficult to see who it is. Winding down the window, the smell of stale smoke tells her.

'Rini, I am glad you are safe.' The words have no ring of sincerity and she wonders what Captain Yorgos really wants to say. 'I suppose that the washing up in the sink was not the first thing on your mind yesterday, so I presume that you haven't come for your money.' It is not a question, it is a statement. 'And of course, today is out of the question, but I expect you tomorrow as usual. The Swiss group have offered to come back. Now, about your mother-in-law...' He begins the new topic before Irini has digested what he has said.

'Actually Yorgos...' She doesn't say the words. Instead, she jerks her chin up, her eyebrows raised, and clicks her tongue in a very Greek *no* before saying, as kindly as she can manage, 'I am sure you will find someone.' And with this, she winds up the window, backs carefully around his frozen posture, and takes the road that goes to the village.

A strange emptiness fills her on the return journey. It feels distinctly odd not to have a weight of debt in her chest. She also has a sense of being directionless after the intensity of the day before. Maybe that was partly what drove Sam to return again and again to Casablanca to do another contract. Maybe that intensity gave him a feeling of purpose. There is also a buoyancy to her mood that she is fearful to give any room to, not sure how it might manifest. In all, she feels disconcerted, and the person who will settle that feeling is Petta. She needs to talk to Petta. Tell him everything. No more secrets.

As she goes in through to the courtyard, she calls, 'Petta?'

'Oh Irini, he was worried sick when you took off. I told him not to worry. He was going to take Theo's moped again. Well, you know me, I am not one to interfere, but on this occasion I told him "no. Give the girl some space, let…"'

'Where is he, Marina?'

'I sent him to the olive grove. I thought a bit of manual labour would take his mind off…' She leaves the word *you* unsaid.

'And Angelos?' Irini looks around. There are no toys scattered over the stone flags.

'He had a play date at Maria's. I thought it best to just continue his days as normal.'

With a hand briefly on Marina's shoulder as a thank you, Irini runs from the house. Her need to speak to Petta suddenly seems urgent. Their olive grove is up past the church and out that way toward the next village. It is not far, but it even crosses Irini's mind to take the car to get there more quickly. Instead, she runs.

The olive grove is an old one and the trees twist up from the ground, the silver blue leaves catching the light in contrast to their black trunks. Marina's great-grandfather planted them, so the tale goes.

An old monastery was disbanded by the church years and years ago and the land that belonged to it was split up and a piece given to each male of the village as a form of aid. This was back in the days when the village was very poor. Marina's great-grandfather acted wisely. Others planted orange trees, which are quicker to mature and give a return immediately. But the olives provide a better income now and will continue to do so for decades.

When they had first moved to the village, in with Marina, the house seemed to echo with every move they made and in their embarrassment, they would come up here for some private time alone together.

There is no sign of Petta. The shade under the olives after being out in the sun all morning is delicious.

'Rini?' His voice comes from the far end, where the olives give way to oranges in the neighbouring piece of land. The leaves of the oranges trees grow much more thickly than those of the olives and that corner is shaded and cool. Hidden from the road, this was always their spot.

'What do you think?' Petta asks, pointing with an old, soil-covered spoon. Irini looks down. Next to his leg is one of the pots of geraniums that usually lives by the courtyard wall. It is empty. The flowers are now planted around the base by the olive tree. Their olive tree.

'It's a reminder,' he says, all smiles and full of his life. 'A reminder that life is beautiful and full of joy.' There it is! The attitude that had made her fall in love with him in the first place. The outlook that turned her world from negative to positive, that brought her to life and enabled her to live again. She cannot stop her smile in response, but it is a smile that does not stay.

This optimism of his has also kept them apart, as he did not want to hear the horrors she has lived through and, she will admit it, she has feared spoiling this aspect of him by filling his head with things he need not know.

His own smile is wiped from his face as she loses hers.

'But mostly, Irini, it is to remind me of the joy of having you. I thought I had lost you yesterday.' There are tears in his eyes. Putting an arm over each of her shoulders, he pulls her into him. 'I have never felt such a devastating sense of loss in my life, Rini. I would have given anything to have taken your place on the boat instead of you. Anything.'

Rini struggles to know how to reply. Where does she begin? How can she explain that being on the boat with the pirate that they shot was actually a wonderful thing? That it has released so much for her. How can she explain what she found in him and through him?

She sits, legs tucked up, her chin on her knees, arms around her ankles, and she fails to sniff away the tears.

Petta sits behind her, pulls her back against him, and rocks her.

'His name was Sam.' Her voice disappears into the leaves that spin and whisper back in the slight breeze. They stay huddled for a moment.

'Tell me, Irini,' Petta whispers back. 'Tell me all about him.' And he reaches out a hand towards the olive tree and writes in the dust.

SAM.

Good reviews are important to a novel's success and will help others find The Illegal Gardener. If you enjoyed it, please be kind and leave a review wherever you purchased the book.

I'm always delighted to receive email from readers, and I welcome new friends on Facebook.

https://www.facebook.com/authorsaraalexi
saraalexi@me.com

Happy reading,

Sara Alexi

Also by Sara Alexi

The Illegal Gardener
Black Butterflies
The Explosive Nature of Friendship
The Gypsy's Dream
The Art of Becoming Homeless
In the Shade of the Monkey Puzzle Tree
A Handful of Pebbles
The Unquiet Mind

38424056R00138

Made in the USA
Lexington, KY
08 January 2015